THE THIRST

NIGEL BOOTON

Copyright © 2024 Nigel Booton.

All rights reserved. This book or any portion thereof may not be reproduced or used in any manner whatsoever without the express written permission of the publisher except for the use of brief quotations in a book review.

PROLOGUE

A dark blue saloon with tinted windows stopped outside the semi-detached house. Two men dressed in grey suits stepped from the car and looked at the property, neither spoke as they made their way up the drive, past the grey hatchback sitting on it. The grass to their right had been freshly cut leaving the smell hanging in the air, and the climbing rose that surrounded the door was in full bloom of red roses.

Both men were over six feet tall with broad shoulders and looked official with their short-cropped hair. The driver pressed the bell and the two waited silently. A neighbour was tendering his garden and keeping one eye on the newcomers. The driver was about to press again when he heard the door lock being opened, followed by the handle being turned.

An elderly man, balding and leaning on a walking stick in his right hand stood in front of them.

'Morning sir,' the driver said looking eye to eye with the elderly gentleman.

'Yes,' was the response in a stern voice.

'Sir you are former detective chief inspector Robert Williams?'

'Yes,' he said, his eyes narrowing a little.

'We are from the ministry of defence; we were wondering if we could talk to you about a case you worked on in the early seventies?'

The old man's eyes narrowed some more; he knew exactly what case they were talking about, it had changed his life and destroyed everything he thought he knew.

'Do you have any identification?' he asked, eyeing the two men standing at his door.

Both men reached into their inside pockets and retrieved a plastic card. The former detective looked over the cards carefully. Their names were on the cards with their photos, but he noticed their ranks and department were missing.

The old man waited a few seconds before turning. The two men stepped up and followed, past the wooden coat stand, that held a long dark coat and a hat perched on top. They followed him past the staircase on the left and turned through the door on the right.

A brown cord sofa was positioned in the middle of the room, in front of a wooden fireplace and a large mirror with photos pushed in the side of the frame was fixed to the wall above. A single chair in the same style as the sofa was placed to the left of the fireplace, positioned in front of the TV that stood to the left of the bay window that was filled with houseplants.

The old man moved over to the single chair and eased himself down, using the stick and arm of the chair.

'Take a seat,' he said, looking at the two men now standing in his Livingroom.

The two sat on the edge of the sofa, scanning the room.

'So how can I help?' the old man asked, removing a hanky from the pocket of his grey cardigan and wiping the end of his nose.

'Well sir, we have read the files from the time, but they are a little vague.'

'Why the sudden interest, and you can call me Williams,' the old man said.

'Thank you, we have been tasked with going over old cases and this one stood out as peculiar.'

Williams didn't believe him, he knew there was another reason for them to drive all the way from London to Yorkshire, but he was too old to care.

'What do you want to know?'

'Anything you can remember.'

The driver removed a recording device from his pocket and placed it on the coffee table.

'You don't mind if we record it do you?' he asked.

Williams noticed his nose had been broken and was a little crooked, he clearly didn't care about it as it had been left to set in its new shape.

Williams shook his head, and the recording device was turned on.

'In your own time,' the driver said.

Williams waited a few seconds before answering.

'Well, this is how I seen it.'

CHAPTER 1

The wheels slid the last couple of feet, bringing the car to a standstill, pushing snow up in front of them. Snow had been falling heavy for most of the day and the dirt track leading to the farm had been covered. The tall hedge that ran parallel with the adjacent field on the right was struggling with the amount of snow that had accumulated on top.

Long wiry fingers pushed the car door open. Out stepped the tall wiry frame of the stranger. Fifty yards ahead on the left was a single farmhouse. The stranger could smell the familiar scent of smoke in the air.

Slowly he made his way down the track that ran off into the distance before disappearing over the hill. He stopped at the wooden gate and looked at the house. A wooden door that had been painted blue and could be split in the middle to allow the top half to be opened, and wooden windows either side of the door stood in front of him.

He pushed the gate open and walked to the door, allowing the gate to close behind him. He lifted the brass knocker, allowing it to fall under its own momentum. The stranger stood, waiting under the concrete canopy that spanned the width of the door. He was about to knock again when the door was opened by a woman in her mid-thirties. She was a lot shorter than the stranger, about 5'2 with brown shoulder length hair. Her blue woolly jumper had a couple of pulls in and her blue jeans had what looked like flour rubbed down the front.

'Can I help you?' she said to the man standing in front of her.

The strangers pale face that was nearly as white as the snow with high cheek bones staired back at her.

'I was wondering if I could use your phone, my car has broken down,' he said in a soft weak voice, after removing his hat.

The man standing in front of her looked cold, weak and tired she thought.

'Come in,' she said feeling sorry for him.

He stepped past her into the hallway. Red tiles showed around a rug that didn't fit the length of the hallway and had faded with time. A single light hung from the ceiling with a glass shade above it, that had discoloured over time. Two wooden doors were on either side of the hallway as he entered, and a set of stairs were to the right.

'It's down here,' she said passing him.

The stranger followed her down the hallway and through a single door at the far end. A solid rugged looking table sat in the middle of the kitchen. Two children were at the table, one standing and one had climbed onto a wooden chair. The two looked at the stranger. He smiled at them. The elder one of the two smiled back. The other gave no response, she just continued to stare.

'It's over there,' she said, pointing over to the left. A green dial phone sat on a Welsh dresser that had plates neatly positioned on the two shelves above.

'Thank you,' he said.

He walked across the red tiles that had continued from the hallway and picked up the phone, placing it to his ear.

'There's no tone,' he told her.

She looked at him and crossed the floor.

'That's strange,' she said pressing the phone to her ear.

'Maybe it's the weather,' she told him, placing the phone back.

'Yes, the snow has probably brought the lines down,' he said, knowing it wasn't the snow that had cut the line.

'My husband will be here any minute, he is just finishing bringing in the sheep, he will take you to the village where you can use the phone.'

'Thank you,' he said with a smile.

'I'll put the kettle on,' she said. I'm Julie, this is my son Adam, he's eight and this is eve, she's three.'

Three and a half Eve promptly said.

Yes, sorry, three and a half her mom said with a smile on her face.

The stranger approached the table and held out his hand. Adam shook the stranger's hand.

'Your cold,' Adam said.

'Just a little, he replied. My name is Tom' he said releasing Adams hand. Of course, Tom wasn't his real name. Over time he had used many aliases but right now, Tom was as good as any.

The stranger held out his hand to Eve. The jester wasn't returned.

'Eve!' her mother said, looking annoyed at her daughter.

'Its fine' the stranger said, drawing his pail wiry hand back.

'I'm going to tell dad,' Adam said, looking at his little sister's face that had flour dotted about that looked like freckles.

The stranger smiled, looking at the table. Crock bowls, rolling pins and different shaped cutting presses were scattered about. A tray of pressed dough that had been cut into different shapes was sitting in the middle of the table.

'We've been making biscuits, you will have to excuse the mess,' Julie told him as she placed the kettle on the gas stove.

'Please, it should be me apologising for the intrusion,' the stranger told her.

'Take a seat,' she told him, pointing to one of the two wooden chairs that were pushed under the table.

'Thank you,' he said, taking hold of the back of the chair and sliding it out.

The chair legs scraped along the floor. Eve placed her hands over her ears to muffle the noise. The stranger sat down opposite her.

'Tea?' Julie asked.

'I'm fine,' he replied.

'It's no bother,' she told him.

'I haven't long eaten,' he lied.

The stranger was thirsty. A thirst that had been building. A thirst that couldn't be quenched with tea, or anything other than what he was thirsting for, and only that would satisfy it, like a junky craving his fix, he knew he should move on, but the thirst was just too much.

CHAPTER 2

The familiar whistle started to build as steam started escaping in greater volume from the boiling kettle. Julie removed it from the gas stove just as the back door was pushed open. A tall figure appeared in the doorway, easily as tall as the stranger. The difference between the two is one of them looked like he was built for the rugged life of farming. Wide shoulders and large hands with nicks and grazes told the stranger he was used to manual labour.

'This is John, my husband,' Julie said looking at the stranger.

'His car has broken down, and the phone line's down too,' Julie told her husband as she placed a hot cup of tea on the table next to the empty chair.

'I can run you into town later,' John said, as he removed his boots by the back door, and hung his coat on one of the spare hooks.

'Thank you,' the stranger replied.

John moved to the sink by the door he had just entered and started washing his hands.

'Did you get them all?' Julie asked.

'No, there's still a couple up by the ridge. I need to take the tractor up; the snow is too deep.'

'Have your cuppa first,' she told him, as she returned to the stove and removed a tray of freshly baked biscuits and placed them on a plate before placing them in the centre of the table.

'Something smells nice,' John said looking at the biscuits.

'We made cookies,' Adam replied.

John sat down next to the stranger.

'Where were you heading? John asked, bit out of the way down here.'

'I was on the main road to York when the battery light started to flash, so I pulled off the main road and seen the smoke from the chimney. I managed to get close before the engine died.'

'There's a garage in the village, but he will be closed at this time.'

'I just need a phone, my son will come and pick me up, that's where I was heading,' the stranger lied to him.

'I'll run you up after I collect the last of the sheep.'

'Thank you.'

'Well let's try one of these cookies,' John said leaning over and picking up the plate.

John offered one to the stranger first.

'No thank you, I haven't long eaten, but they do look delicious,' he said looking at the two children.

Eve and Adam both had a smile on their faces from the compliment they had just received. John circled his hand over the plate, glancing at his two children, that were watching with great enthusiasm as to which one he would choose. He picked one from the centre before placing the plate between his two children.

'And its time you two were getting ready for bed,' Julie said.

'But its only just got dark,' Adam complained.

'I know, but you have to get up early to feed the sheep and collect the eggs before school,' she told him.

'Don't look at me, you heard your mom,' John said.

'It's not fair,' Adam mumbled to himself as he pushed the chair back under the table. Eve followed Adam out of the kitchen, but not before they both chose a biscuit.

'Children, want to burn the candle at both ends,' the stranger said.

'Getting them up in the morning is even harder,' Julie said as she started to collect the utensils from the table.

John finished the last of his tea and stood.

'May I come with you?' the stranger asked. I have never been in a tractor before.'

John looked a little taken aback by the request.

'Why not, Julie said, there is loads of room in the cab, he takes the kids with him all the time.'

'If you want,' John said slipping his feet into his boots.

The stranger stood and joined him at the back door as John removed his green wax jacket from the peg.

'I need to get the tractor from the barn,' John told him as they stepped outside.

The stranger smiled and nodded.

The snow was light and fluffy under foot, leaving deep impressions as the two walked across the yard. A stone outhouse stood on its own to their left and wooden fencing ran from the outhouse across the yard and turned ninety degrees back to the corner of the house.

John lifted the latch to the gate and allowed the stranger through before closing it behind them.

The barn stood on its own to the right. The roof had sunken slightly in the middle, pushing some of the slates up. Two large wooden doors that had seen better days were closed and some of the snow had been blown up them. The fields in the distance looked like a freshly washed quilt had been thrown over them and drifts of snow had come to rest halfway up the stone walls that separated the fields.

'It's just over the ridge,' John said pointing his finger to where the land seemed to suddenly stop and disappear.

'What's over there?'

'It drop's down into the valley and climes up again. Some of the sheep have settled under some trees. It's too slippery for the 4x4 and I can't leave them out all night, not in this.'

The two stopped at the barn doors. John lifted the wooden latch from its holder and allowed it to hang. A large bolt had been used to allow the piece of wood to turn three hundred and sixty degrees. Like most things on the farm, it was mend and make do. The stranger helped pull the barn door open.

'That will do, John said as a space big enough for them to enter was made, the tractor will do the rest.'

The two stepped inside. A beat-up tractor stood in the middle, near the front, and hay bales were stacked at the rear. The place was cold but dry and the bales were stacked like stairs running up to the roof. The small amount of light that was seeping in from the door didn't matter to the stranger. His vision was as good in daylight as moonlight.

Finally, the stranger had what he wanted. He was alone, in a secluded place and his senses were on overdrive.

He could see the blood pulsing through the veins in John's neck. The excitement was too much to bear. He knew it was forbidden, but the thirst was too much to contain any longer.

CHAPTER 3

Julie had finished washing the last of the utensils.
'I hope you two are ready for bed,' she said as she climbed the stairs.

She heard the familiar sound of scurrying feet moving about the bedrooms. She stopped at the top of the stairs to the familiar sound of giggling. She stepped into the door at the rear of the hallway. Eve was lying in bed waiting for her mom. She stepped from the bare floorboards of the hallway onto the green carpet of her daughter's bedroom. The brown zigzag wallpaper was broken with a couple of posters and an old wooden wardrobe stood to the right. Julie passed the bed that was directly in front of her and closed the curtains.

She picked up two books and showed them to Eve. Eve pointed to the one with animals on the front. She placed the second book back on the table at the foot of the bed and spent ten minutes reading to her daughter until she fell asleep. Julie kissed her on the forehead and closed the door as she left, leaving her looking cosy and comfortable.

She stepped into her son's room. Adam was sitting up reading the book he had brought home from school.

'Time for lights out mister,' she said with a smile on her face.

Adam didn't argue. He handed the book to his mom and lay down. Julie placed the book on a set of draws behind the door and kissed him on the forehead.

'Night mom.'

'Night, see you in the morning,' she said, still with the smile on her face. She switched the light off, plunging the room into darkness. She listened as Adam got comfortable before closing the door.

Julie placed the kettle on the stove and readied three cups and a teapot for when the two returned. She removed some flour from one of the overhead cabinets and made some fresh dumpling for the stew she had made that day. The children had eaten, but she had waited for her husband to finish his days tasks. It was their time to spend together. She placed the dough balls in the stew and placed the lid on. The biscuits were placed on a blue willow pattern plate and placed in the middle of the table. Three bowls were placed on the table and a tray with milk and sugar was also placed in the middle. She looked out of the window to see the barn doors open but no sign of them.

She decided to add a couple of logs on the fire in the Livingroom, there was a film on that evening she wanted to watch, that's if they could get a signal on one of the three channels.

CHAPTER 4

John was confused and in pain. He was trying to figure out what had just happened. He had placed one foot on the tractor when he found himself flying through the air. He lay on the ground, his left side hurting from the fall. He watched as the stranger approached. Johns whole body was lifted from the floor. Before he could react, he was once again being hurled through the air, with the tractor being his new destination. His chest hit the side first and his legs ricocheted off the rear wheel. The impact knocked the wind out of him, and his left shin bone snapped in two. He fell back to the ground, the pain from his leg excruciating. John tried to pull himself under the tractor, but before he made the few feet, he felt his right ankle being pulled into the air.

The stranger had total control of his prey. He bent down grabbing the back of his pray with his right hand. His prey was hurled into the air once more. This time John landed near the top of the haybales. With one leap the stranger had landed next to him, grabbing his shoulder and sending him hurtling to the ground, the twenty feet or so below.

The stranger looked down at the man who had offered to help him. His body lay disfigured, but there was no remorse from the stranger. With one leap he landed at the bottom of the haybales and walked slowly to his prize. He grabbed him by the ankle and dragged him back to the haybales.

John was unable to move. His body broken and battered, and he felt himself being lifted onto the haybales, unable to do anything he watched as the man that had come for help unfasten his long black coat. What he seen next sent a shiver down his spine. This weak feeble looking man's face started to disform. His lower jaw started to protrude forward followed by his upper gums. His eyes had changed to black, a cold dead black with no life in them.

The stranger opened his new jaw line, two sets of fangs, as sharp as needles and as white as snow, protruding from his newly formed jawline. He fixed his eyes on the artery that was pulsing in John's neck. The strangers vision meant he could see through the skin and pick out the blood oozing through the veins like a river of gold.

John felt the pain as the stranger sunk the pearly whites into his neck. The stranger had pushed his head to one side and was feasting on him. Unable to do anything about it, he lay there, thoughts of his family running through his head. Slowly a peace and quietness enveloped him, so much so that he started to forget that the life was being slowly drained away from him.

The stranger stood upright, blood dripping from his mouth and down his chin. He stumbled onto one of the haybales, his legs weak as the new life-giving blood was starting to take effect. He knew it would take five minutes to gain the full effect. Until then he knew he was vulnerable. He had learned from other's mistakes over the centuries, he had made sure his pray was isolated and alone.

The stranger stood tall next to the lifeless body. All the blood and moisture had been drawn from the gaunt waxy looking body that lay in front of him. The stranger fixed his coat and dusted himself down. He had no feelings for the man that had offered him help. No more so than a tiger would that was feasting on the carcass of a fresh kill.

The stranger stepped out of the barn. The snow had stopped falling, and the stars were shining bright in the sky. The stranger turned and looked at the house. The kitchen light was on, but the rest of the house was in darkness. He strode with a newfound enthusiasm as he closed the gate to the yard at the rear of the house. He stopped at the rear door and peered in, it was empty, he opened the door and stepped in closing the door behind himself. Julie had finished with the fire and returned to see the stranger standing at the back door.

'Good your back,' she said looking over his shoulder to see where her husband was.

The stranger smiled at her before undoing the buttons down the front of his coat. He removed his coat and hung it on one of the hooks, before turning to see Julie placing the kettle on the stove.

CHAPTER 5

Three days later a ford Granada stopped at the front of the isolated farmhouse. A constable stood at the front door. Detective Chief Inspector Robert Williams had been given basic information from dispatch. Williams closed the passenger door and made his way to the front of the farmhouse. Three days ago, it looked like a picture postcard, but the heavy rain had washed the idyllic scene away.

'Sir,' the young constable said as he stepped aside.

Williams and his sergeant stopped at the door.

'Who's the woman?' Williams asked nodding to a woman standing fifty yards away.

'Don't know sir, she turned up about ten minutes ago.'

Jackson, go and see what she wants,' Williams told his sergeant.

'Sir,' came the reply.

Williams stepped through the front door.

'Down hear,' a familiar voice called out.

Williams walked down the hallway and stopped at the open door to the kitchen. Before he could speak a bright flash filled the room. The police photographer was snapping at what looked like a body lying on the kitchen table.

Williams walked around to join the doctor.

'Go and find somewhere else to do that,' Williams said looking at the man with the camera.

The short stubby man got the message and left the kitchen and headed upstairs.

'Wow, how long has she been here,' Williams said looking at the dried-up corpse.'

'Now that's the conundrum the tall lanky figure of the doctor said.'

'What do you mean?' Williams asked, looking at him.

'The local farmer popped over this morning because he hadn't seen them for a couple of days and found them. He said he was over a few days ago drinking tea with them.'

Williams hadn't missed what the doctor had said.

'What do you mean, them?'

'One in the barn and two children upstairs, all looking the same.'

Williams stood up straight, scratching the back of his head.

'You don't look like this after a few days,' he said pushing his hand towards the corpse.

The doctor raised an eyebrow and opened both his hands.

'Do we know how she died?' Williams asked.

'Not till I get them on the slab for sure.'

'Best guess then?'

'It looks like all the fluids has been drained from them.'

'They all the same?'

'Yes.'

'I'll take you down to the barn,' the doctor said picking up a black case from the floor.

The two stepped passed another constable at the entrance to the barn. Both doors had been opened wide. Williams could see the second victim laying on the haybale at the rear, his leg and arm hanging over the side.

'He's the same as the one in the kitchen,' Williams said standing next to the corpse.

'Told you.'

'One difference, this one has a broken leg,' the doctor said pointing to the hanging leg.

'You ever seen anything like this before?' Williams asked.

'Never,' came the reply.

'They look like they have been mummified,' Williams said leaning in closer to the corpse.

'Like I said, I have never seen anything like it.'

Williams stood straight, rubbing the side of his face. The expression told the doctor he was baffled too.

'Any idea how it was done?' Williams asked looking at the doctor.

'I have absolutely no idea, this is out of my league.'

'Come on George, give me something.'

'I wish I could Robert, come on, it gets worse,' he said turning and leaving the barn.

The doctor climbed the stairs to the bedrooms with Williams behind. The two stepped through the door and stopped. The corpse of a little girl lay covered with a blanket. Williams could see from the top of her head that the same fate had befallen her.

'Another one in here,' the doctor said opening the door. Neither of them entered.

'No sign of a struggle.'

'No, they look like they were asleep when it happened.'

'When what happened?'

'I'll be able to tell you more later.'

'Don't give me the, I've got a back log,' Williams said looking eye to eye with him.

The doc shook his head, 20:00,' he replied.

Williams nodded. The two knew this wasn't just one of the run of the mill cases. A whole family had been killed and Williams knew it wouldn't be long before the local papers and radio got wind of it. That would mean he would be under pressure from up-stairs for a fast result.

Williams left the doctor and made his way outside. Jackson was talking to the crews of a couple of ambulances that had arrived.

'Jackson! Williams shouted.'

Jackson made his way over, dodging the many puddles of water that had filled the large potholes, landing in one of them wouldn't have made much difference, Williams could see the heavy rain had soaked through his coat and the bottom of his trousers were the same.

'Did you speak to the woman like I asked?'

'Yes sir, she wants to speak to who's in charge.'

'Don't tell me, she's a reporter.'

'She wouldn't say or give her name.'

The two stood, looking up the track at the single figure, rain running off the brim of Williams's hat.

Williams didn't say anything else. He pulled his collar up to protect himself as best he could from the driving rain and headed for the woman in the distance.

CHAPTER 6

Donna wade had her coat pulled tight as she stood watching the scene unfold in front of her. If the information was correct, then the horror that lay in the house wasn't something she had ever seen before. She had been told stories and heard folklore, but never actually seen it.

She watched as the man that had entered the house on arrival was now heading in her direction. She also knew that if it's what she thinks it is, then he will laugh at her and think she is a crank or mentally disturbed.

'My sergeant said you wanted to speak to me,' Williams said, as he stopped in front of her.

She was dressed in black trousers; black boots and she had a thick dark grey coat with the hood pulled up, protecting her from the weather.

'I may have some information about what took place,' she said in a quiet voice.

'How so?' Williams asked.

He was suspicious of someone who claimed to have information. Usually, people who have information are involved in some way. He waited patiently, he could see she was thinking how or what to tell him.

'You're going to think I'm crazy with what I have to tell you.'

'Why would I think that, look if you have any information about what took place, then you have a duty to tell me.'

Donna took another few seconds before she said it.

'I don't believe you are dealing with things of this world.'

Yep, a crack pot he thought. But maybe she also knew more than she was letting on, maybe involved in some way, and she was his only lead.

'Would you like to elaborate on that,' he said playing along with her.

'Do you believe there are things in this world we can't comprehend?' she asked.

'We don't know everything,' he replied.

'Do you believe in God?' she asked.

'I'm somewhat of a religious man.'

She noticed his green eyes had narrowed and he held eye contact. She knew what she said in the next few minutes would determine whether he thought she was crazy or maybe he would want to talk to her again.

'So, you believe in God without any proof, is that correct?'

'I guess.'

'Then with that, you must believe that the devil is real too?'

Where is she going with this, he thought.

'I'm listening,' he said.

'The bodies are all dried up, mummified,' she told him.

'You have been in there!' he said.

'No.'

'Then how do you know?'

'Someone informed me.'

'Who?'

'I don't know.'

He knew he didn't have enough to hold her, but he didn't want her disappearing too, she knew more than she was letting on.

'Are you staying local?' he asked, changing his tone.

'I haven't had time to book into an hotel.'

'There's a nice one in town, we will give you a lift.'

She knew he wasn't offering the lift out of kindness, he wanted to know her where abouts. But to get out of the rain, she had to accept he was suspicious of her, and she needed him if she was going to prove what she had come here for.

'Thank you,' she said.

The two made their way to his car, both dodging the potholes. Jackson opened the rear door, allowing her to throw her haversack in first.

Williams didn't continue the questioning, partly because he didn't want Jackson to know what they had been talking about, and partly he didn't want to frighten her off.

Jackson stopped outside the Regal hotel. Black metal railings ran across the front, and seven stone steps led up to the entrance. Jackson opened the rear door. She thanked him and joined Williams on the kerb.

'I know the manager, get you a good room,' he said.

'Thanks.'

The two entered through the revolving door. To their right, comfortable chairs had been placed and people were sitting and drinking. The reception desk was to their left, their wet shoes squeaked on the polished marble floor.

Williams flashed his badge and asked for the manager.

'Sorry sir, he's off today,' a young woman in her early twenties told him.

'We need a room,' he told her.

'A double sir?' she asked.

'Single will be fine,' donna said.

The receptionist turned and removed a key that was hanging on the back wall.

'I will need some details,' she said and passed over a piece of paper.

Williams waited until she had filled in the form, taking note of her full name, date of birth and address.

Donna passed the form back and received the key in return.

'You're on the fourth floor, room forty-eight,' She also gave her the standard information about what time breakfast was and evening meals plus the general layout of the hotel.

'I will let you settle in, and we will talk later,' Williams told her before she headed to the lifts.

Williams closed the car door and removed the radio from the glove compartment. He passed on the information about Donna wade and wanted all relevant information.

'Who is she sir?' Jackson asked.

'Not quite sure yet, but she knows something she's not letting on.'

'Why not drag her in?'

'She may clam up… no, softly softly first. I think she wants to tell me something, but she doesn't know how. Drop me back at the station, then I want you and a couple of flat foots to go around the local farms and villages to see if anyone as noticed anything out of the ordinary.'

What does she know and how does she know it was all that was on Williams's mind as they made their way to the station.

CHAPTER 7

Donna exited the lift and found her room. She placed the key on a dressing table to her left and dropped the haversack on the single bed. A single chair was placed under the dressing table, she ignored it and opened the door she had passed. Standard bathroom and clean she thought. She moved to the window where a single set of draws had been placed under. The rain was still beating down and didn't look like slowing any time soon.

She removed her coat that was soaked through and hung it over the back of the chair. She knew what she needed to do before she could sort out her hair and clothes that had started to soak up the water where her coat couldn't hold back the rain any longer. She opened the haversack and removed a small notebook. She sat on the chair, careful not to lean on the sodden coat.

'Hello,' came the response from a woman's voice as she held the phone to her ear.

'I need to make a call,' Donna replied.

'You need to dial nine then your number,' she was told.

'Thank you,' Donna told her and placed a finger on the receiver.

She waited as the phone rang out. Not only would it be the first time she was close to something she had worked on for most of her adult life, but the person she was contacting had only seen photos himself.

'Hello,' came the voice of her mentor and confidant.

I've made contact,' Donna told him.

'Don't tell me, he thinks you are mad and dismissed you as a crank?'

'No, he is suspicious of me, thinks I'm involved in some way.'

'So, the information was correct then.'

'Seems so, when I explained about the condition of the bodies, he asked me if I had been in the house.'

'Excellent, whatever you do, don't give him cause to dismiss you as a crank, this could be the proof we have been looking for.'

'But as soon as I tell him, that's exactly what he will do.'

There was a silence for a few seconds.

'First thing to do is arrange a neutral location, just the two of you, don't go straight in with the information. Did you ask him if he was religious?'

'Yes, he said somewhat.'

'Good, use that against him to keep him interested, remember, as soon as he thinks you're a nut he will dump you and then we will be out the loop.'

'You mean string him along?'

'No, stringing him along would mean we are deceiving him, what you are doing is waiting until he is ready to believe the full explanation.'

'Ok.'

'Remember, keep him interested.'

'I'll try,' she said, before re-placing the receiver.

Donna removed a skirt and a jumper from the haversack. She stood in the steaming shower, thinking how she could keep the detective hooked. No doubt he would be sceptical to say the least. She turned under the steaming water and allowed the water to soak into her hair. But she wasn't interested in her look, she had spent too much time and energy to blow the chance to confirm their existence.

She dressed in the clothes she had placed on the bed and headed down to reception. It had been an early start and she had skipped breakfast.

'Hi, do you do afternoon food?' she asked the girl that had booked her in.

'No, sorry, breakfast and evening meals only,' the young girl told her.

'What time does evening meals start?'

'Five-thirty.'

'Do I need to book?'

'Yes.'

'Can you book me in then please.'

'Sure, there is a café at the end of the road, they do breakfast all day,' the girl told her.

Donna looked at the large clock hanging on the wall. Another four hours before she could eat at the hotel. Even her slight build would need food before then.

'Thanks, I think I will pop down.'

The young girl bent down and retrieved an umbrella. Donna thanked her as it was handed over.

'Turn right, it's at the end,' the young girl said pointing to the revolving door.

Donna huddled under the umbrella as the rain bounced off it. She was still lost in thought of how best to handle the detective.

She passed a newsagents and a men's clothing shop. The door to the cafe was positioned right on the corner. A small bell hung above the door that rang as she entered. The café was typical of its time, Formica tables, lino for flooring and the counter at the rear, and the smell of cooking oil in the air.

The plump woman didn't say anything just smiled and waited. A serving hatch behind her showed a man and two women busy preparing food.

'Could I have a ham sandwich and a tea please?' Donna asked.

'To take out,' the women asked, her brown hair perfectly permed Donna thought.

Donna looked around. A couple of tables were empty.

'Eat in.'

That will be £1:24 please.'

Donna opened her purse and handed over two one-pound notes.

The woman rang up the total on the large cash register. Donna listened as the cogs and wheels moved in unison and the total popped up on three large white signs.

Her change was handed over with the receipt.

We'll bring it over, the woman said before turning and relaying the order through the hatch. The woman behind the hatch nodded her head but didn't stop what she was doing. Donna retreated to a table that was one away from the window. She stood the umbrella against one of the chairs and waited, the only thing on her mind was how she would deal with the detective.

CHAPTER 8

Williams was sitting at his desk. The thought of what he had seen that morning baffled him. He had seen plenty of murder scenes, but never with the bodies that way. The off-cream radiator made a gurgling sound that broke his train of thought. He looked up to see Jackson heading his way.

'Still raining,' Williams said looking at Jackson, his hair flat to his head and his coat had no doubt leaked through.

Jackson didn't reply to the comment. He removed his coat and hung it on the peg, revealing Williams was correct about the coat.

'We've been to every farm and spoken to everyone in the village, no one has seen any strangers in the last week, Jackson told him as he sat at the desk opposite.

'I hate these sorts of cases, no leads, no physical evidence, and no suspects, what are we supposed to do with it?' Williams asked.

'What about the woman that was hanging around?'

'She knows more than she is letting on for sure,' Williams said standing and heading to the window.

'Why not just pull her in?'

'Because if we play hard ball she will clam up, and I want to know her background first.'

Jackson waited and watched as the DCI stood staring out the window. He had witnessed it hundreds of times.

'Wright, I want you to get a couple of them, he nodded to the incident room that was full of detectives, either sitting on the phones or going through paperwork, to chase up this Donna Wade. At the moment she is our only suspect.'

'Yes sir,' Jackson said leaving him alone.

Williams knew stranger murders were the ones that had a high chance of not being solved. Most murders are perpetrated by someone known to the victim. He also knew the murders would probably be on the front of the local newspapers in the morning, plus local radio. That would bring the super on his case, that was partly why he hadn't pulled Donna in. If the heat got too much from upstairs, he could always pull her in and report they had a suspect in custody. He didn't figure her for it, but he knew she was holding back when they spoke.

It had been hours and Williams had spent most of that time going over the cases that would soon be in court.

They were slam dunks for him, but he was a dot the I's and cross the T's detective.

'Sir we have that information you wanted on Donna wade.'

Williams leaned back in his chair.

'She has no former convictions, works as an assistant to a Professor Myers at Oxford university, who specialises in history.'

'And?'

'That's it.'

What would a history assistant from oxford be doing up here poking around in a multiple murder case? Williams said. He wasn't asking for Jacksons opinion he was just speaking his thoughts.

'Come on, we need to go and see the doc, now you have dried out. Williams noticed Jacksons hair had become wavy and wasn't its usual slick with a side parting.

'I was hoping to get off sir?' Jackson replied.

'Me too,' Williams said, as he put his coat on.

Jackson didn't bother pleading, the date he had for that night would have to wait.

The two stopped at the side entrance to the mortuary. The single-story building had been purposely positioned away from the sight of the visitors and patients of the hospital. The place everyone knows exists but doesn't want to acknowledge.

The two walked down the path between the grass lawns, stopping at the blue double doors. Jackson pressed the bell, and the two stood in silent.

They were invited in by the doctor. Williams and Jackson followed, down the long dull corridor. They turned left at the end, through another set of double doors. A long window on Williams's left showed him that four trollies were lined up, all covered with white sheets. The white tiles on the walls and chrome utensils and work surfaces combined with the smell of disinfectant gave the place a cold and sterile feel.

The doc stopped at the trolley on the left and pulled the sheet down to the waist, exposing the brown dried up corpse. The two looked at it as the doc retrieved a clip board from the table behind.

'I can honestly tell you, in all my years, I have never had the privilege,' he said holding the clip board against his white coat.

Williams looked at him.

'First things first,' the doc said, looking at the clip board.

'This is John Walters, aged thirty-nine, cause of death, the doc looked at the corpse, Hypotension I suppose.'

'Plain English doc,' Williams said.

'The sudden drop in blood pressure caused his heart to fail.'

'But what about all this?' Williams asked, pointing to the skin.

'Basically, he has been dried out like a prune.'

'How?'

'Well, if you look here, hold on,' the doc turned and placed the clip board down and put on a pair of surgical gloves. He turned the corpses head to the side.

'You see, two puncture holes leading to the Jugular Vein.'

Williams and Jackson moved in for a closer look. They looked at the two holes that had broken the skin about two inches apart. They leaned back as the doc turned the head back parallel with its body.

'But why would someone want to do that.,' Jackson asked.

'That's your conundrum, mines the how, not the why,' he said pulling the sheet back over the corpse.

'The other three are the same, do you want to see?'

'No thanks,' Williams said.

'My full report will be with you tomorrow, I have contacted my old tutor from London college, he and a professor are coming to take a look, if there is anything else?'

'No.'

'You can find your own way out I take it?'

'I think we can manage,' Williams said as he watched the doc retreat to his office to the right.

The two sat in the car.

'Where too?' Jackson asked.

'You know what, take me home, we'll come at it again in the morning.'

Jackson was relieved. His date had been blown out, but at least he would be home before midnight.

CHAPTER 9

A car horn sounded outside. Williams stopped and fixed his tie in his hallway mirror. His grey suit and thin black tie reflected his mood. As soon as he woke his thought were on the family. It wasn't the image from the morgue, it was what had taken place at the farm.

Williams closed the door to his three-bedroom semi-detached house that he lived in alone.

'Where too sir?' Jackson asked, no morning or greeting.

It was 08:00 and Williams had questions that needed answering.

'By the way, there are a couple of reporters at the station waiting to speak to you,' Jackson told him.

'Let's not go there then… hotel, I have some questions for miss wade.'

The local radio skipped to its usual news bulletin. The murders were the first thing reported. Their sources had described how a whole family had been murdered on a remote farm and the police were unavailable for comment.

'Looks like the circus has started,' Williams said turning off the radio.

'We knew it was coming,' Jackson said as he pulled away from the kerb.

Williams sighed, 'I was hoping we could get half the day done first.'

The two continued in silence. Jackson parked directly outside the front of the hotel, the double yellow lines not bothering him. The two climbed the steps and pushed their way through the revolving door and stopped at the reception.

'Can I help you?' a middle-aged man dressed in the company suit and a black dickie bow asked.

He stood behind the long reception desk that was still trying to hold onto its Victorian look.

Williams flashed his badge. 'I want to speak to miss wade.'

'I will just find out what room she is in sir?' he said, giving Williams that half a smile that said he was a bit nervous.

She's in room forty-eight Williams told him.

'I will ring up sir, may I say what it concerns?'

The guy waited for a response.

'No,' Williams said bluntly.

He knew the guy was just being nosey and Williams wasn't in the mood to accommodate him or his request.

The guy picked up the phone. Williams could see the disappointment on his face of not being in the loop.

'We'll be over there,' Williams said, nodding to the vacant seats opposite.

Williams and Jackson sat and waited. It was a good fifteen minutes before she stepped out of the lift. The two detectives stood and watched as she made her way to them.

'Going somewhere?' Williams asked as she was dressed in the coat that had clearly dried out after yesterday's downpour.

'Breakfast.'

Don't they do breakfast here?'

'It's very busy she told him, and you want to talk about yesterday.'

'There's a café on the corner,' she told him and headed for the revolving door.

Williams and Jackson followed her out onto the street.

'Jackson, wait here,' Williams told him.

Jackson nodded, disappointed he had been sidelined. Not for the questioning, but he could have just done a bacon and egg sandwich.

The two walked down to the café, neither felt the need to start the conversation. They both knew what was coming, but they both had different agendas. Donna ordered tea and toast, just a mug of tea for Williams, it was too early for food. Williams paid for both and the two sat to the side of the counter. They had any seat they wanted as the place was empty. Williams spooned a full sugar in his drink and stirred, Donna took it as it came.

'You haven't brought me here to buy my breakfast,' she said placing the cup in front of herself.

Williams placed the spoon down.

'You said you have information for me,' holding eye contact while waiting for her response.

'You said you are a religious man.'

What's with the religious thing again, he thought.

'What's that got to do with yesterday?' still holding eye contact.

'Everything,' she knew he was waying her up with the constant gaze.

She broke the eye contact and picked up the tea.

'Look, like I said yesterday, if you know anything it's your duty to tell me.'

'Do you believe in the devil?' she asked.

'What?'

He knew she had something to tell him, but what, and with all the religious questions he couldn't figure out. Does he play along or right her off as a crank.

'Logic said if you believe in God then you must believe in the devil.'

She could see she was starting to lose him.

Williams took a sip of tea as Donna's toast was placed on the light blue Formica table. Williams slid the ashtray to one side and removed a packet of cigarettes from the inside pocket of his grey overcoat. He lit one up as donna spread butter on the toast.

She's got until he finished his cigarette then he was done with her.

'I'm listening,' he said, leaning back on the chair.

He felt the back of the blue plastic chair give a little. He waited for her to finish the first mouthful of toast.

'The bodies, they were all dried up, like looking at thousand-year-old mummies,' she said.

She noticed he made eye contact again.

'Go on,' he said taking another drag from the cigarette.

'But they died only a few days ago, how could that be,' she kept eye contact with him.

Did she go for full disclosure and risk losing him, but only giving him some of the information could also lose him.

'If I'm correct, I know how they were killed.'

Williams didn't respond, he finished the last of the cigarette and doubted it in the ashtray.

'Come on then,' he said standing suddenly.

She didn't understand, was she being arrested or taken back to the house. She had no choice but to follow. The two walked in silence back to the car. Williams opened the rear door for her and then climbed in the front.

'The station,' Williams told Jackson.

Jackson looked at her through the rear-view mirror with a slight smile on his face as he started the car.

CHAPTER 10

The stranger was sitting, watching the light fluffy clouds moving across the sky. The grey gaunt look had been replaced with one of a much younger man. He still sported the pale skin, but at least he felt invigorated, thanks to the family he had just visited.

The old farmhouse that sat on its own on the edge of the Yorkshire-moors was in bad repair. He had used it for over fifty years and made no repairs over that time. The remoteness it gave him was perfect. He knew however that with the start of the new estate being built in the next valley, it would only be a matter of time before he needed to move on.

Over the centuries he had become a custom to moving around. He stood from the table that was covered with cobwebs and dust. A family of mice were scurrying around between the walls, not like it bothered him. Animals of all description gave him a wide berth, not like humans that had the uncanny and annoying ability to think he was approachable. He couldn't understand how they had lost their six-sense to know when there is danger about.

The bare floorboards squeaked as he made his way from the Livingroom to the door in the hallway. He opened the door and started to descend the stairs to the basement. The pitch black would have caused humans a problem, but not him. A light bulb wouldn't have made no difference, It wasn't like he could have switched one on, as the property didn't have the luxury of electric or running water that humans seemed to rely on these days. How they had become dependent on things he couldn't understand.

An old barn door four-foot wide and eight-foot long lay in the middle of the floor. He pushed it to one side exposing a hole big enough for him to lie down. The soil was cold as he lay, pulling the board back over himself. He needed to rest, even though it had been a couple of years since he had felt this good, he knew a short rest would only improve his strength. The thirst that had returned would need quenching again, and very soon.

CHAPTER 11

Jackson parked at the side entrance to the station, the door gave a straight entry to the holding cells.

'Leave the engine running,' Williams told him.

'Sir,' Jackson said,' it wasn't an ok, it was more of a why.

Williams opened the rear door for Donna to exit.

'Get in the front,' he told her.

Jackson and Donna looked at each other over the roof of the car. They both thought they would be going straight to an interview-room.

'Get in,' Williams told her as he seen a couple of reporters heading in their direction.

'No comment for now,' Williams told Jackson as he closed the door and reversed out onto the main road.

'I thought you were arresting me,' Donna said.

'I did think about it, and to be honest, I don't know how you are involved, for now.'

'I'm not involved with the deaths.'

'We'll see.'

She turned her head back from him, at least she wasn't in a cell, she thought.

'Where are you taking me?' she asked.

'You said you could tell me how they died, convince me or you will be in a cell by the end of the day.'

'Why do you think I have anything to do with it?'

He didn't figure her for it, she didn't have the size or strength to do what he had seen in the barn. The farmer was a big strong man that was used to physical work. But something in the back of his mind told him she had answers that he needed. He also had no other suspects or witnesses, so whether he liked it or not he was keeping her close.

Williams parked in front of the morgue.

'You're joking,' she said staring at him.

'You said you knew how they were killed.'

'I'll just tell you; I don't need to see them.'

'Let's go,' he said opening the driver's door and exiting.

He waited a few seconds before she exited the car. The calm questioning demeanour from the café had been replaced with apprehension. It would also allow him to gauge her response. He needed to know was she involved, did she really have answers, or had she just gotten information from someone and was enjoying the ride.

The two strode over to the door, donna just behind. Williams pressed the bell and waited. The wind was pushing Donna's hair across her face, so she held it back with one hand. Williams didn't comment.

'Back again detective,' the doc said holding the door open.

'You can take my report with you, save me sending it over,' the doc said before walking back down the long corridor with Williams and Donna behind.

She felt the heartbeat in her chest quicken with every footstep. She had never seen a dead body before and all she could think of was don't pass-out. They rounded the corner and passed through the double white doors and stopped as the doors closed behind them.

'Pull out the male from yesterday,' Williams said looking at the doctor.

'Who's this?' he asked, looking at donna.

'Consultant,' Williams said looking back at her.

The doc looked a bit puzzled, but he didn't bother pushing the issue. The truth is, he wasn't really bothered, the lead detective brought her so what did it have to do with him.

'Follow me then,' he said.

The two followed him through another set of double doors to the right of where Donna was standing. The wall to their right was filled with grey and chrome doors, all just big enough to take a body. The doc stopped at the end of the wall and opened the last one in the middle row. Donna followed Williams and stood next to him. She watched as the body was slid out, covered in a white sheet.

Williams gave the doc a nod for him to peel the sheet back. The doc obliged, folding it down to the waist. Donna stood staring at the prune like corpse laying in front of her.

Williams turned his head and waited. He could see she was lost in the moment, her eyes fixed on the leather like skin that had sunken against the skull.

'Well?' Williams asked.

The sudden noise jolted her out of the trance she had gotten lost in.

'Yes,' she said looking at him.

'There are two puncher holes in the neck,' she told him, not looking back at the corpse.

Williams stared at her for a couple of seconds before nodding to the doc.

'Glad to be of service,' he said sarcastically, not like I'm busy is it,' he mumbled pulling the sheet back and pushing the body back in.

Williams didn't respond, he turned and left, collecting the report. He waited until they were sat in the car before he spoke.

'One of two things is going to happen, you either tell me what you know, or I'm taking you back to the station and you will have plenty of time to think about your answer's.'

'You won't believe me; you will think I'm a nut job.'

'Humour me.'

'Do you promise to listen constructively and with the evidence too.'

'Go on.'

It was all or nothing she thought, hopefully with the report he had from the doctor it would give her a fighting chance.

'You remember what we spoke about in the café about God and the Devil, good and evil,'

He didn't respond.

'What killed that family wasn't something from this world.'

He sat waiting, an old interview trick, when someone's talking, don't interrupt.

She waited for his response but didn't get one.

'The thing that came calling was a Vampire. I know you don't believe me but look at the evidence. All the evidence is in the report you are holding, everything I have told you is backed up by that report.'

She waited, there was nothing more she could do, she had laid everything on the line in that moment.

'You expect me to go to the chief constable and the press and tell them we have a Vampire on the loose?'

'They would just laugh at you, I know.'

'You're dam right they would, quickly followed with the sack, and then the men in white coats.'

'But look at the evidence,' she nodded to the folder he was holding.

'If you won't believe me, or the evidence or what your eyes tell you, come and talk to the professor I work with.'

Great, a nutty professor too, he thought. He couldn't believe he was even entertaining the thought of what she was saying. But what he had seen with his own eyes and the report did corroborate what she was telling him.

'And where is this professor?'

'Oxford.'

He handed her the folder and reversed out. Why was he doing this. Everything he knew told him the whole story was rubbish. But something in the back of his mind made him curious.

CHAPTER 12

The journey down to Oxford was laborious. Williams couldn't believe he was even contemplating the idea. But it did have one bonus, he wouldn't need to answer to the reporters.

They exited the motorway and started crawling along the narrow roads. The closer they got to the centre, the more elaborate the buildings became. Williams could see why it had gotten its name of the city of spires. The skyline was filled with towers and steeples in the Gothic theme. A lot of roads were still cobbled the closer they got to the centre. Donna directed him along a narrow road between a tall brick wall on either side. She instructed him to park on the left. The two walked to the end of the street. Suddenly the place seemed to be busy with students, some on foot, but most on cycles dodging in and out, no real order.

The two turned left along the yellow brick wall. They stopped at an old wooden gate that came to a point at the top, enclosing the space made for it. A single door was recessed in the larger gate that donna stepped through. A man dressed very smart in a black suit and bowler hat exited what looked like a small room to their right.

'Good afternoon miss Wade,' he said touching the brim of his hat.

He looked at Williams with his round face and barrel belly.

'You have a guest, I will need your name sir for the visitor log,' he said in a deep voice.

'Robert Williams.'

Before he could say detective donna interjected, 'he's here to see Professor Myers.'

'Very good sir,' he said turning and heading back into his little hide away.

Williams didn't comment on the interjection, he figured she didn't want anyone knowing he was a detective, maybe too many awkward questions.

He followed her along the stone path that ran around a perfectly manicured square lawn that dominated the centre of the open space. Old wooden windows that were slightly deformed in shape due to the building being old and leaning slightly were on their right. Rose bushes that had been cut back and were showing their thorns sprang from the soil beneath the windows. The building directly in front of them was much the same, except it was larger and more grandeur. Both buildings on either side of the main building looked like they were added later. Four stone steps led up to a double doorway with solid wooden doors, the right one being held open by a solid looking latch.

A large wooden staircase was directly in front of them, wide enough for six people to stand shoulder to shoulder. They climbed the stairs before turning back on themselves to finish the climb to the first floor. Paintings of what William's thought were former heads, hung on the walls, all donned with the customary robes and hats. Williams followed along the oak floorboards that had turned dark brown with age before stopping halfway down the corridor. Donna opened one of the doors on the right.

'I didn't expect you back so soon,' Williams heard as he followed her in.

'Professor, this is the detective I told you about.'

Williams stepped from behind her and saw an elderly gentleman sitting behind a large oak desk. One half filled with books that had bits of paper protruding from the tops, the other half had folders that were under a brass lamp that looked like it had been sitting there since the invention of electricity. The professor stood, his gold rimmed glasses sitting on the end of his nose. He looked immaculate in his tweed suit with matching waistcoat.

'Pleased to meet you,' he said holding his fragile hand out across the desk.

Williams wasn't here for the niceties, but he didn't want to be rude, so he accommodated the professor with a handshake.

'Please sit,' he said gesturing to the two comfortable chairs that would look better suited to be sitting in front of an open fire.

'I've told him,' Donna said as the two sat.

'And let me guess, he doesn't believe you, yet here he is.'

Williams didn't answer. The professor was right, here he was, sitting in the study of an Oxford professor, following the trail of what he could only describe as a fantasy story at best.

The professor stood and made his way over to the bookcase that filled one side of the room. He removed a large book and returned to his seat. He flicked through until he came to his desired page. He turned the book and pushed it across the desk, leaving it sitting in front of Williams.

'What am I looking at?' Williams asked looking at the two pages of elegantly scrolled writing?

'It started in 1639 in Weston Russia. A kingdom had been under attack from northern tribes. Slowly the northern tribes had been gaining strength and it seemed that the final onslaught was all set. In desperation the lord asked the devil for help as God would not get involved with man's affairs. But there was a price to pay. The lord asked what the price was, but the devil said first we need to save your people. The lord, looking at defeat accepted, and three days later the northern tribes were defeated with such ferocity that some of the survivors said it was like facing an army of wild beasts. After the battle the lord waited to see what the price was, but the devil never came for his penance.'

'What's that got to do with the four corpses I have?' Williams asked.

'A few years later the lord took a wife, and when she gave birth, the devil came for payment.'

'Don't make deals if you don't know the price to pay,' Williams said.

'I agree, the professor said, Donna could you turn the light on please.'

The room was starting to get dark, late afternoon was turning into early evening. The small brass circle hanging from the ceiling that held five lightbulbs lit up, illuminating four of them.

'That's better, I will continue. The lord racked with guilt and pain begged God for help. God agreed to protect the child as it was innocent. But he could not help the lord or his wife. The lord begged for his wife to be protected, but God said, you should have told her from the beginning, her pain is on you.'

'I still don't know how this helps me,' Williams said again.

'I'm coming to that.'

The professor sat back in his chair that made him look too small for it.

Once the child was born the devil came for his prize. Realizing that God had put the child under his protection the devil was fuming. He cursed the lord and his wife. They would not die, or be able to eat or drink again, they would only be able to quench their thirst by drinking the blood of humans. All the fighters in his army were cursed too. On hearing this the lord's wife, in despair, ran at the devil. The devil used a broken branch that pierced her heart and turned her to ash.

'And you expect me to believe this fantasy?' Williams said.

'You have four bodies that prove it,' the professor replied.

'Tell me, were they bled dry?' the professor asked.

'Yes.'

'And were their two puncher holes in the necks, the site of where they were drained?'

'Yes.'

'Yet you are still in denial of what your eyes tell you, because you can't explain it with what you have been taught.'

The professor stood and moved to an oil painting hanging on the far wall. He pulled the right side and swung it away exposing a safe. He removed a brown envelope and returned to his seat. He removed what looked like old photos and shifted through them like a pack of playing cards.

'These were taken in the late 1800s.'

Two grainy photos were placed on the desk. The professor turned on the table lamp, but it didn't help with the clarity. The professor raised his finger and returned to the safe. He removed a black leather holder and unzipped it.

'The bodies were as dry as dust and had the look of old leather, the coroner's report from 1889.' He placed another photo down, this time a little bit better than the first two. Williams could clearly see that the bodies looked like the four he had at the morgue. Six photos were placed directly under the previous ones.

'These were all taken during the second world war, he placed two more coroners reports down.

'They say the same as the first one.'

'You see, your bodies are not the first, and they won't be the last, or are they unique.'

'I need to sleep on it,' Williams said.

'Yes, I was the same in the beginning, all I had been taught, told me it was impossible, but the more I dug around the more I uncovered, until finally there was enough proof to convince even an old sceptic like me.'

'Where did you get all this?' Williams asked.'

'The first ones I brought by accident; they were tucked away at the back of an old painting I brought. So, I showed them around and was put in touch with a dealer that delt in, shall we say, specialist merchandise.'

Williams looked at the professor.

'Anyway, over the years little bits pop up now and again.'

'He has his own folder in the car,' Donna said looking at Williams.

Williams stood, 'it's been a long day and I need to think,' he told them.

'Why don't you stay the night, it's getting late, a long drive back,' the professor told him.

Williams figured he wasn't bothered about his well-being but more interested with the coroner's report. But he was correct, it had been a long day and the drive back wasn't something he was in a rush for.

'You could stay with Donna; I stay on site you see.'

Donna looked at the professor and then back to Williams.

'No, it will be fine, I will find an hotel,' Williams said.

He didn't want to stay with his only suspect, too complicated.

'I will meet you both here tomorrow, 10:30.'

'Very well,' the professor said, standing and holding out his hand.

Williams obliged and nodded to Donna. He needed time to think, he also needed to inform the station of his whereabouts.

CHAPTER 13

The door knocked. It was Williams's 08:00 call he had asked for.

The room was small, but the window that was built into the roof gave a good view of the road below. Williams made his way down the steep stairway to the first floor where the communal bathroom was positioned. February wasn't tourist time so most of the hotel, well pub one would say, only had a couple of guests present. Williams had asked for the top floor; he knew how places like this could get rowdy.

He had tried not to think about what the professor had said and the evidence he had provided, but no matter how he tried to put it out of his mind, he was always drawn back to it.

The one of two bathrooms was basic, clean and adequate without the frills like upmarket hotels. The floorboards squeaked under the flowery carpet as he made his way back to his room. It wasn't ideal but he hadn't planned on staying, his clothing would need to make do for another day. Not ideal but needs must, and he had endured worse.

He was seated by a well-built lady, probably in her forties. He ordered the full English and retrieved one of the newspapers. The front page was dominated with a picture of the Prime minister Edward Heath and Britain's entry into the European Economic Community. He turned to the back pages; politics wasn't something he cared about.

The woman that seated him returned with a tray and placed a pot of tea and sugar bowl down, followed by a small amount of milk in a matching jug to the cup and saucer. He thanked her and placed the paper on the side of the table.

He could see the tea was strong as he poured. A gentleman that was sitting two tables down was tucking into his food. Williams figured he was a traveling salesman; he didn't give the impression of someone from one of the universities. The wooden beams that held the ceiling had bent slightly over the years and the wooden floor that looked original was slightly leaning to the bar. The dark wood and pictures gave the place a welcoming feel.

His breakfast was delivered with toast. The food was tasty if a little on the small side, but overall, the bed was soft, the food enjoyable, and the proprietors were welcoming. If he ever decided to return, he would stay again.

He thanked them for his stay and exited the front door. The street pathing was narrow, only allowing two people to walk side by side. He started the stroll back to the university, bicycles speeding past and groups of students with scarfs pulled tight hurrying, maybe late for classes. The walk would help him to clear his head and think of what had been discussed. He past the row of shops that had been turned into tourist premises, better business than the students he thought. He stopped at the corner. The road to his left had what looked like dwellings, he crossed the road and kept walking. The brickwork was elaborate, and the spires gave the place a feeling of old England.

The wooden door to the university was open. The guy that had taken his name yesterday was standing in his doorway.

'Good morning, Mr Williams,' he said.

Good memory Williams thought.

'I'm here to see the professor again.'

'I will call and let him know you have arrived.'

He turned and left Williams standing just to the left of the doorway as students rushed past.

A few seconds past when Williams heard his name being called from the first-floor window. The professor was hanging out waving him over.

Come up come up was being shouted as he made his way to the entrance. Williams climbed the stairs, and the professor was waiting for him outside his room.

Williams could see the joy on his face has he held out his hand.

'Come, sit,' the professor said holding on a little too long.

'Donna not here yet,' Williams asked as the two sat.

'You're a little early, I was hoping we could put the evidence that you have, against what I have,' the professor said.

Williams could see he looked a little disappointed that he hadn't arrived with it.

'I have a few questions first, like how did donna know about the murders?'

'I got a phone call.'

'From whom?'

'Don't know, I was given an address and told it might be of interest.'

'Who knows what your side interest is?'

'It's not something I shout about, as you can appreciate.'

Williams could understand that. But someone knew what had taken place in that house, and they didn't feel the need to inform the police.

'So, you don't know anyone that knows about what you do, except Donna, yet someone called to inform you of what had taken place.

'Correct.'

'Man or woman?'

'Man.'

'Anything else, accent, foreign, English?'

'English,' the professor said, nodding his head, as if confirming it to himself.

'Yes, definitely English.'

'Reginal?'

'Not really, I would say very plain, I'm sorry, not very helpful.'

'I don't know, now I know that a Man, English, was in that house after the murders and definitely before the police, its more than I had before I arrived.'

The door knocked.

'Yes,' said the professor, looking up.

Donna stepped in, closing the door behind her. She had had the luxury of showering and changing. Williams noticed that she had changed from trousers to a knee length skirt and matching grey jumper, slightly lighter than the coat that she was wearing from yesterday. Her hair was hanging loosely, and he detected a hint of makeup, very subtle, but some.

'Donna, good morning, I wondered if you would be so kind and collect the file from the detective's car, so we can compare notes?'

Williams looked at the professor. He hadn't agreed to it, the professor was taking it upon himself to presume.

'That's if its ok with you,' the professor said, reading Williams's face.

Williams waited a few seconds before handing over the keys. He waited until donna left before continuing.

'You see, I can't figure out how you and Donna are involved in all this.'

'Like I said, were not involved, we were given information, that's all. Do you really think a sixty-four-year-old professor and a twenty-eight-year-old woman could do what was done to that family.'

Williams conceded the point. There was no way, even if the two of them were working together would they have the physical strength.

The professor removed the file from the safe and placed it on the table, just as donna returned. She handed Williams the file followed by a parking ticket. Williams took it from her and stuffed it in his inside pocket, just after he let out a sigh. Williams could see the professor hadn't taken his eyes from the file since it had entered the room.

Williams stood and placed the photos of the farmer and his wife on the desk. The professor immediately joined them. The three stood staring at the two corpses.

'You see, the exact same,' the professor said, not taking his eyes from the photos.

'I thought there were four?' the professor said looking at the file.

Williams removed two more. Donna left the desk, Williams understood, he didn't like looking at them too, but it was his job, like it or not, he was stuck with it.

Williams retrieved the photos and placed them back in the envelope.

'let's say you're right, how do I catch him, or it?'

The professor returned to his chair.

'Why don't I explain on the way.'

'On the way to where?' Williams asked.

'The crime scene of cause.'

CHAPTER 14

The Three of them joined the motorway. The professor had a grin like he had just won first prize in a raffle. Donna sat quietly in the rear, the large back seat looking too big for her. The Granada was a large car by most standards and its big v-six engine ate up the miles.

'Is this what it feels like to be on the hunt for someone?' the professor asked.

'How does it feel?' Williams replied.

'Exciting, I've never thought of going out into the field before.'

Williams didn't reply. He knew what the professor felt. He had had the same feeling his first time. He remembered being the driver to his old guvnor, like Jackson his to him.

The miles rolled on and Donna hadn't said a word. She looked afraid sitting up against the door behind the professor. Maybe she was thinking what if they do meet up with him or it. If it's as dangerous as the professor says, then maybe she has every right to be apprehensive.

Williams stopped at the services, he needed to fill up and they all needed a comfort break.

They re-joined the motorway. Williams couldn't believe he had two passengers in toe. He had decided to keep them far from the station, anything they discussed would need to be done far away from anyone.

'It's very quiet and secluded,' the professor said, looking at the landscape as they made their way from the motorway and along the country lanes.

'Gods own country,' Williams said.

'Yes, I can see that.'

'There are the dales, north Yorkshire moors, guy Fawkes was born in York too, and don't forget Yorkshire pudding.'

'How could we forget such a delight, I was thinking more of the fact that if you wanted to hide, this would be the perfect place.'

'Lots of farms, many abandoned.'

'I think we may be in the right place,' the professor said.

'Do you know how big Yorkshire is?' Williams asked.

'No.'

'Well let me tell you this, if he has gone to ground, we will never find him.'

'I don't think he will.'

'Why do you say that?'

'It's like an addict, now he has had his fix, I bet he won't be able to control it.'

Williams looked in the rear-view mirror, 'what do you think?' he asked looking at Donna.

'I think the professors right, the temptation was too great in the beginning, and now he has feasted, I think he won't be able to stop himself.'

'So, there is going to be more bodies,' Williams said looking back at the road.

'Afraid so,' the professor said looking across at Williams.

'Why now?'

'Maybe he has been in a state of hibernation.'

'And what if he goes back into hibernation?'

'He won't,' said the professor.

'You sound very sure.'

'Why would he, look around, he has the perfect hunting ground.'

'All the story's say they can't come out in daylight, Williams said.

'There not stories, most nursery rhymes derive from some truths. Take ring a ring a roses, that comes from the plague. Then there was Mary Mary quite contrary. According to some, it's about queen Mary the 1^{st,} or bloody

Mary as she was better known, for the execution of hundreds of protestants, and by the way, silver bells and cockle shells were actual torture devices, not gardening tools, so some say.'

'Most old saying come from part truths, they get changed over the years, or some of the meanings get lost, but most are rooted in past deeds of some sort.'

Williams didn't say anything, he knew the professor was probably right.

'I'm going to drop you at the hotel, I need to check in at the station, I will come back as soon as I can.'

Williams stopped outside the Grand.

'You ok with the cases?' he asked before they got out.

'I'm sure we will be fine,' the professor said, before closing the door.

Williams waited until they went inside, it wasn't like they were going to disappear. He had excluded them from his investigation, there was no way they could have done what he had seen. The truth is the more he thought about it, the more he started to believe what Donna and the professor had told him.

CHAPTER 15

Williams parked at the side of the station. Before he could open the door, two reporters were asking questions through the closed window. Good afternoon or was it early evening. The light was fading fast, and a photographer was snapping away, his flash temporary blinding Williams.

'As soon as I have any news, I will let you know,' he told them, closing the door.

'Rumours are, something strange took place up there,' said the women reporter.

Williams knew her, over the years he had gotten some useful information from her and given her a few scoops along the way, but this was different. He couldn't explain any of it, plus if he told her about his two new helpers, he would be out of a job before he got past the front desk.

Williams stopped and turned to her, 'Look as soon as I have anything concrete, you will be the first to know, and stop with the rumours, you're better than that.'

'Robert, I need something for tomorrows edition,' she told him holding out a cassette recorder and mike.

'Sorry, too early.'

She had always used his first name, maybe she thought being more personal would get more info. But Williams knew how they worked, loyalty and the truth wouldn't get in the way of a good story.

Williams climbed the three steps and entered through the front. The desk Sargent immediately came to the window on seeing him.

'You're wanted,' the Sargeant said, looking at Williams with a look that said sorry to be the bearer of bad news.

'I figured so.'

'He's not happy with you taking off like that.'

'Following leads.'

'Tell him, not me.'

Williams climbed the stairs to the second floor. He turned right along the corridor, the walls were shoulder hight, then frosted glass to the ceiling. The blue square carpet tiles had faded over time as Williams stopped and knocked the door that said superintendent on a wooden plaque with gold writing.

'Yes,' came the reply.

Williams entered; a metal desk sat to the right with filing cabinets behind and shelving ran the length of the room to his left.

'Close the door,' the super said, dropping his pen on the file he was working on.

'Enjoy your little trip, did we?'

'Following leads sir.'

'And what leads were they?'

'I needed to exclude someone from the investigation.'

'And?'

Williams wasn't asked to sit; he knew it wasn't one of those chats.

'The person in question had nothing to do with it.'

'And you had to go all the way to Oxford, wouldn't a phone call have been enough.'

'I needed to corroborate her story.'

The super waited a few seconds.

'So where are we on the farm thing?'

'To be honest sir, back to square one.'

'Well, I haven't had the privilege of looking at the file, because someone took it with him.'

'It's in the car, do you want me to fetch it.'

'No, I want it on my desk first thing, with a report of why you went to Oxford and where we are.'

'First thing sir,' Williams replied.

The inspector picked up the pen. Williams knew the conversation was done. He closed the door on his way out. He had had his butt kicked and the report was his way of punishment.

'How did it go?' the sergeant asked, his two arms leaning on the windowsill.

'I think if you look close you can still see the boot marks on my ass.'

'You know he likes being kept in the loop.'

The sergeant was in his fifties, and he had seen Williams come through the ranks.

'Do me a favour, tell Jackson I will pick him up in the morning, it's been a long couple of days.'

'Will do, and by the way, the coroner has been looking for you.'

'What for?'

'I don't know, I'm not your answer service.'

Williams nodded his head, 'I'll speak to him tomorrow.'

'You two, the sergeant said, catching two constables that had just entered.

'I need you to go and speak to a woman that's called in, she thinks someone has been snooping around her house.'

CHAPTER 16

Donna and the professor were seated at one of the tables. They had checked in and washed before coming down for dinner. The long dining room was grandeur and two large chandeliers hung from the ceiling and large doors that would have been opened in the summer led out onto a large patio overlooking mature grounds.

'What do you think he's going to do?' Donna asked. She had waited until the young girl had taken their orders before asking the question.

'Who?' the professor asked.

'Williams.'

'I have no idea, I've never been on an operation before, it's exciting don't you think.'

Donna looked at him, doesn't he understand, if they do track him down, how are they going to stop him, more importantly what will happen to them. The professor sat in his dark blue three-piece suit taking in the surroundings. Donna looked on in disbelief that he looked lost.

The starters were delivered, homemade vegetable soup and a crusty cob.

Williams had flashed his badge at the reception and was shown through to the dining area. He thanked the lady and made his way to the far corner.

'I see you didn't wait for me,' he said, standing next to the table.

'We weren't sure if you would be back this evening,' the professor said placing his spoon down.

'Sit, join us, the soup is very good,' the professor told him as he wiped his mouth.

Williams sat next to Donna, directly opposite the professor.

'Look I have a job to do, I'm not going to be around during the day.'

'We understand,' Donna said.

'How this is going to work, I don't know,' Williams said glancing around the room.

'Well, while you're busy, donna and I will make our own enquiries.'

'Hold on, I don't want you two disappearing all over Yorkshire asking questions that could get you noticed, because it could lead straight back to me.'

'Don't worry we will be discreet.'

Williams turned and looked at Donna. She raised an eyebrow as if to imply she couldn't control him.

'Are you going to join us?' the professor asked again, before placing his spoon in the empty bowl.

'No, I will grab something on the way home, I have to write up a report.'

'Nothing to do with us, I hope,' the professor said leaning back in his chair.

No, he lied, he knew if he hadn't gone to Oxford he wouldn't be sitting there now. He also knew he wouldn't be running two very different investigations on the same crime.

'Glad to hear it,' the professor said.

'I suggest we meet back here tomorrow evening, 19:00, ok?'

'Sounds good to me, we can pool our findings,' the professor said.

Williams nodded his head.

'I have a question?' donna said.

The two looked at her.

'Let's say we find him, then what do we do?'

Williams and the professor looked at each other.

'We will cross that bridge when we come to it,' the professor said.

Williams didn't argue, it was a valid question, one that he hadn't thought of.

'Maybe that's something you two can figure out, you're the experts,' Williams told them. Maybe it would stop them traipsing all over Yorkshire getting up to who knows what, he figured.

'Anything else?' Williams asked, looking at donna.

'Ok, tomorrow at 19:00 then,' Williams said leaving them alone.

Williams stopped at the fish and chip shop on his way. Not having a wife and the long hours meant he visited the place at least a couple of times a week.

The house was dark and looked uninviting as he parked on the drive. He knew it was going to be a long night and he needed to concentrate. The typewriter wasn't his favourite thing, and he knew it was his punishment for his trip to oxford.

CHAPTER 17

08:00 and Williams parked at the side of the station. It was four in the morning before he finished the report. He had showered but didn't have time to get rid of the two-day stubble.

He walked past the front desk with the report under his arm. The incident room was quiet, and Jackson hadn't arrived yet. What he was more concerned about was what the professor and Donna would be doing. He figured he could trust Donna, but the professor was a different story.

'Morning sir,' Jackson said stepping through the open door to the office.

'Don't bother hanging your coat, I want you to take a couple of officers and go back up to the village and go and question everyone again. I want to know if anyone seen anything out of the ordinary at least two weeks before the bodies were found, this wasn't some random attack.'

Williams leaned back in his chair. 'The place must have been staked out,' he said.

Jackson was going to ask about his trip to oxford but decided against it. He left Williams sitting on his own.

The phone rang. Williams answered it and listened.

'Thanks,' he said replacing the receiver.

Williams climbed to the second floor and knocked the superintendent's door and waited.

'Come in,' came the response.

Williams entered, not too sure how he would be received.

'Tea?' said the super.

'Yes please.'

Williams was expecting a hostile reception. The change from yesterday had thrown him a little.

The super placed a cup and saucer on the desk.

'Sit down, that the report?' he asked, nodding to the file Williams was holding.

'Yes sir.'

'Good.'

The super held out his hand. Williams passed the report and sat. The super retrieved his coffee and sat opposite Williams. The two sat in silence. Williams waited, watching as he turned the pages, referencing the report with the coroner's report and photos.

'What do you make of it?' he asked, not taking his eyes from the photos.

'To be truthful sir, I have no idea.'

'I can see that; I've never seen anything like this before.'

'I've sent Jackson and a couple of detectives back to the village to re-question everyone.'

The super didn't respond, he re-examined the coroner's report.

'What's with the puncher wounds in the neck?'

'The doctor thinks that is the site where they were drained from.'

'What are we going to do about the press?' Williams asked.

'We say nothing, I need to make a few calls, see how they want to play this.'

'They being?' Williams asked.

'They being well above both our pay grades.'

Williams understood. How could they explain it, they needed to keep a lid on it. Williams knew it was only a matter of time before one of his officers passed on the information for a few quid.

'Ok leave the press side of it to me,' the super said closing the file.

'Sir.'

'I want to be kept informed on this one.'

'Yes sir.'

The super placed the file down on the desk. Williams stood knowing the meeting was over. At least he hadn't received another dressing down.

Williams closed the door and headed back down to his office. The files that were ongoing wasn't going to be looked at, not until he had closure from the new case. A few criminals were going to get an easy ride, at least for a while. He decided to ring the hotel where Donna and the professor were staying.

'Good morning, the Grand hotel, how may I help?' came the response.

'Could I talk to one of your guests please, Miss donna wade,' Williams said.

'Do you know what room sir?'

'forty-eight.'

'Just one moment.'

Williams could hear muffled voices.

'I will put you through now sir.'

Before Williams could thank her, the phone started ringing.

'Hello,' came Donna's voice.

'Morning, just seeing what you two are up to today?'

'You mean checking?'

'Just making sure you don't get into any trouble.'

'I don't know what he has planned.'

'Well, just keep him out of trouble, this is an active investigation.'

'I'll try.'

'Good, I will see you tonight at 19:00 then.'

'Ok,' she said before the phone went dead.

Williams placed the phone down. A feeling in the pit of his stomach told him it wasn't going to end well.

CHAPTER 18

Donna's hotel door knocked. The professor was standing there in his khaki three-piece suit and his glasses showing from his front breast pocket.

'Ready?' he said leaning on his cane.

'Where we going?' she asked.

'Well, breakfast of cause.'

Donna knew that breakfast was only the start of the day. The two made their way down and sat. A young girl came and took their orders.

'We need to find somewhere we can hire a car,' the professor said.

'I was thinking how we were going to get around,' she replied.

'I was hoping the detective would help us with that one, but he has his day job I suppose.'

'We need to be independent of him,' Donna said.

'Your right, come at it from two different angles.'

'Thank you,' they both said as their breakfasts were placed in front of them.

'I don't get a fry up very often,' the professor said has he cut into a sausage.

Donna smiled as she cut into her poached egg, thinking he was treating it like a holiday. After they had finished, they made their way to the front desk. The gentleman that had booked them in yesterday was working on some paperwork.

'Could you tell us where we could hire a car from?' the professor asked.

'There's a local business close to the city, he may be able to help. If you turn right out the front and keep going, it will be on your right, about a ten-minute walk. I could order you a cab if you like.'

'No no, a brisk walk would do us good,' the professor said.

The two exited the hotel and started the walk. Donna couldn't help thinking, it was more of a stroll than a brisk walk. Maybe the professor had forgotten he had slowed with age. She didn't say anything, he had earned his stroll.

The brisk walk that should have taken ten minutes had taken closer to twenty. The residential properties had started to change the closer they got to the city. Just as they were told, a forecourt that looked empty except for two cars and a van was on their right. A brick building to the side that would have been a residential property, but had been changed into part of the business, stood in bad repair. The two climbed the three steps and entered through the main door. A counter ran the width of the room and a round man sat behind.

'Good morning,' he said with a soft voice.

'Morning, Donna replied, we were told you hire vehicles?'

'We do, how long for?'

Donna looked at the professor, 'couple of days,' he replied.

'I can do that,' the round man said pulling himself from the chair.

'Need some paperwork.'

He leaned down behind the counter, the bending exposing the bald spot at the back of his head that he had tried to hide by combing his hair back.

'Sightseeing?' he asked, placing some papers down.

'Yes,' donna said before the professor had any chance to answer.

Donna did as requested and filled in the paperwork and handed over her driving licence.

'No points,' he said, handing her back the paper licence.

The three exited the building and made their way along the road and through the double gates. They stopped next to a beige Vauxhall viva.

'She has a full tank, just return her with the same,' he said.

He opened the driver's door and got in. He pulled the manual choke out and started it up.

'She's as good as gold, he said pulling himself out. Just give her full choke in the morning, you won't have a problem with her.'

Donna thanked him before he left them to it.

The two got comfortable before Donna reversed away from the eight-foot wire fencing that ran around the forecourt. She inched to the road holding the steering tight as the wheels bumped up and down over the loose gravel.

'Which way?' she asked stopping at the road.

'Right, back passed the hotel,' the professor said, his attention being drawn to the radio in the dashboard.

Donna did as she was instructed.

'So, what's our plan?' she asked, changing into second gear with a slight crunch.

'I thought we would go and have a look at where it took place.'

'But he said we were to stay out of their investigation.'

The professor turned on the radio and proceeded to turn the dial, watching the red line move along.

'There, that's better,' he said, as music started coming from the single speaker.

Donna glanced across at him.

'It will be fine; he won't even know we have been there.'

She concentrated on the road ahead. Everything Williams had told them had gone out of the window.

CHAPTER 19

The walky-talky crackled as it lay on Williams's desk. It was soon followed by the voice of Jackson.

'Go ahead,' Williams said holding it.

'Sir we have a problem up at the farm,' Jackson said followed by more static.

'Can't you deal with it?'

'They said I am to contact you.'

'Who?'

'The two people I found snooping around.'

Williams's heart sank. He knew exactly who it was, the talk last night clearly went straight over their heads.

'Keep them there, I'm on my way.'

'Sir,' came the response, followed by more crackling.

How was he going to explain it. First, he didn't know what they had said, if they had told Jackson everything, that was going to take some explaining.

The sergeant had called him as he passed the front desk, but he had ignored him. The two reporters that were hanging around immediately approached as he stepped out of the station. No comment was all they got as he sped off.

Damage control was the only thing on his mind. The ten-minute drive had given him time to come up with a couple of ideas. But deep down he knew if they had spilled the beans on why they were there, he was in trouble.

Williams pulled up behind the two cars that were parked next to the farm. He could see two people sitting in the back of the squad car, with Jackson leaning on the roof. He came to meet Williams.

'Sir, they said you know them.'

'Did they say why they are here?'

'No, they wouldn't say anything except to contact you.'

Williams was relieved, at least they had kept their mouth shut.

'Yes, I do know them.'

Jackson was waiting for an explanation, he stood looking at Williams. He wasn't going to get one, not before he had spoken to them anyway. Williams strode over to the back of the car and opened the door.

'Out,' he said to both.

Donna exited first, followed by the professor. Donna didn't look at him as she stepped away from the car. The professor on the other hand had started to explain before he had even exited. Williams shut him down immediately, Jackson was too close for the sort of conversation that was to be had.

'Over there, Williams told them,' Pointing to the gate that led to the farmhouse.

'I will take it from here,' he told Jackson.

'Don't you want me to run them in Sir?' Jackson asked.

'No! I said I will take it from here.'

'Did you speak to the locals again like I asked?'

'Yes sir, one of the farmers said he spotted a car parked up a couple of days before the incident.'

Williams waited.

'And!' he finally asked looking annoyed that he needed to ask.

'He said it was a darkish colour but couldn't tell the make or model.'

No help at all Williams thought, but at least if the super asked, he would have something to tell him.

'Ok, head back to the station while I deal with these two.'

'How do you know them sir, Jackson asked looking at the two standing by the gate, isn't she the one that was here when the bodies were found?'

Williams was being backed into a corner and he needed to think fast.

'Yes, they are researching rural life for the university.'

Why he had said that he didn't know. He could see Jackson looked puzzled by his response, but it's all he could think of to explain why they were there.

'Is that their car?' Williams said, trying to change the subject.

'Yes Sir,' Jackson said looking over to it.

'Good, they can make their own way back to town then.'

'You mean you're not going to run them in?'

'Did they enter the property?' Williams asked, hoping they hadn't.

'No sir, when I pulled up, they were standing where they are now.'

'Then they have broken no laws have they.'

Williams was relieved. Donna may have kept stum, but the professor would have spilled why they were there for sure.

'I guess not,' Jackson said, looking annoyed that he couldn't drag them back to the station.

'What do you want me to do now sir?' Jackson asked.

'Head back to the station and type up what the farmer said about the car he seen, at the moment it's all we have.'

'I'm going to give these two a piece of my mind and send them on their way,' Williams told him before watching him drive away.

Once Jackson had disappeared, he made his way over to them.

'What the hell do you think you are doing!' he asked.

His tone made sure there was no way they could misinterpret his annoyance.

'It was my fault,' the professor said looking like he had had a dressing down.

'I don't care who's fault it is, you can't go interfering in an ongoing investigation, what part of that don't you understand!'

Donna didn't say anything. The look she gave Williams was enough to tell him she had no choice in the decision to come to the farmhouse.

'Look, Jackson is already suspicious of you, he said looking at donna. With him catching the pair of you hear, next time he won't report it, he will just bring you in.'

'I'm sorry,' the professor said.

'Good! don't let it happen again or I will have to send you back to oxford!'

'While we are here, could we take a look inside?' the professor asked.

Williams couldn't believe what he was asking.

'No! and there is nothing to see, the bodies have been taken to the morgue.'

'Yes, that was the next thing I was going to ask.'

'Don't bother,' Williams told him, I will meet you both at 19:00.'

Williams walked away. He was annoyed at them, but he was also annoyed at himself for allowing them to get involved. All his years of experience told him to send them back, but something in the back of his mind told him he needed them.

CHAPTER 20

'I told you we shouldn't have come,' Donna said as the two walked to the car.

The professor waited until they were both sitting before answering.

'I think we should head to the local pub,' he said as he clicked in his seat belt.

'Why?'

'It's afternoon and most of the farmers will be in by now, that's where we will pick up most of the gossip.'

The professor placed his stick between the seat and door. He sat waiting for Donna to come up with a reasoned argument not to go. He knew she always made good arguments, that was one of the things he liked about her. But she didn't protest.

She stopped the car at the end of the dirt track.

'Which way?' she asked.

'I think it must be left or we will be heading back to the city,' he said waiting patiently.

Donna did as instructed. The car trundled along with the sound of classical music coming from the speaker. The professor looked like he was enjoying the moment.

'See,' the professor said pointing to a sign that told them they were one mile away from the village.

Donna slowed as she passed a small church that had a waist high wall and a wooden gate and archway, that had twisted slightly with age. Dead ahead was the village. The road split in two just in front of her. The road to the left had six houses on either side before giving way to unkept hedges. Donna took the right fork, passing a post office and shop that had wooden boxes outside filled with a variety of vegetables. An iron Mungers was the final shop before they gave way to more houses. Donna past them and the houses on her left, heading to the pub that was situated at the far end of the village.

The pub had been positioned slightly away from the road, allowing cars to park out front. The oak beams were marked and twisted with age, and the lead windows had started to lean slightly. Donna parked in the first spot available.

'We need to be careful what we say,' Donna said as she killed the engine.

We are tourists,' the professor replied, removing his stick from between the door and seat.

The two walked along the front to the entrance that had a stone frame around it. Dark wooden floorboards that hadn't been level for a long time and a low ceiling led to the bar. The place looked cosy the professor thought.

'What can I get you?' a man of about sixty with brown metal framed glasses asked.

The professor looked at the choice of ales available from the drafts in front of him.

'I will take a half of stout please,' the professor said before looking at Donna.

'A pot of tea if possible? driving.'

'Sure,' the landlord said nodding his head.

'If you take a seat, I will bring them over.'

The professor paid before heading to the far end where a fire had been lit.

The professor stopped at a vacant table just before the fire. Two men had taken the one next to it, exactly what the professor would have done if he was in first.

'Good afternoon,' the professor said to them as he removed the chair.

The two nodded at him but didn't speak.

The professor removed his tweed jacket and placed it on the back of the chair before sitting.

'I'm sorry to bother you, but on the radio, it said there has been a murder locally.'

Donna sat looking at the back of the professor's head, she couldn't believe he had asked that question.

The gentleman sitting nearest the professor turned slightly to him.

'Yes, and it's not the first,' he said.

'What do you mean?' the professor asked, looking like he was aghast.

'I have lived here all my life, and I can tell you there has been some strange goings on.'

'Don't listen to him,' the barman said placing a tray on the table with their order.

'You explain what happened to that family then, and the things I have seen over the years.'

'The things you have seen, always after five or six pints,' the barman said looking at him.

'I'll be proven right one day, you'll see, mark my words.'

'Enjoy your drinks,' the barman said before leaving.

The professor took a sip of the stout. 'Very smooth,' he said as he watched Donna pour the tea from the teapot.

The professor placed the glass down and turned. 'What did you mean, strange goings on?' he asked starting the conversation again.

'Who are you?' the second of the two men asked, eyeing him with suspicion.

The professor knew he needed to ease their worries, if he was to get any information from them.

'We are up from Oxford for a few days, sightseeing is all.'

'Years ago, an old couple were found dead in their home under strange circumstances, we were never told what had happened, but folks from London came up and took the bodies with them.'

'Really,' the professor said looking intrigued.

'Then there was that night I was walking home, the guy had turned and was sitting side on his chair, leaning over the back. Well, I could see as clear as if it was daylight. I swear he leapt across the field bounding on all fours, each leap must have been twenty feet or so.'

'Your joking the professor said,' When someone is in full flow don't interrupt.

'And then there has been the livestock problems, ask Davie,' he said looking across at his companion.

The guy's friend wasn't so forth coming as his mate.

'You have had a few problems yourself then?' the professor said trying to prise any information he could.

'A few sheep have been taken over the years,' he said.

'Tell him what they were like when you found them,' as if his story would corroborate his own.

'It was foxes,' he said.

'Well, I don't know any foxes that would do that,' he said.

'Do what?' the professor asked, picking up his glass by the handle and taking a long sip.

'There was nothing to see,' the second guy said staring at his friend with a stern look.

The first guy got the message. He picked up and finished the last of his drink before leaving.

The professor knew the conversation was over. He smiled at the second guy before turning back to Donna.

'We need to make a move,' he said before downing the last off the stout.

Donna reversed back onto the main road, heading for the city.

'That second guy didn't look to impressed,' Donna said.

'Locals don't like strangers prying into their business.'

'What did you think of the first guys story?' she asked.

The professor waited a few seconds before answering. 'I think we are definitely on the right track, and in the right place.'

Donna continued the drive back to the city, she knew the information they had gotten from the pub backed up their suspicions, but what next. The professor hadn't thought of anything but finding the culprit, or the possible consequences if they did find him.

CHAPTER 21

Williams watched the clouds building in the distance. It was how he felt about the professor and Donna being there, he knew somewhere along the line they were going to get too deeply involved and it was going to come back to bite him. He also knew that he had no authority to send them back to Oxford, after all they were civilians, and free to come and go as they pleased.

He slowed as he approached the station. Just has he thought, the two from the local paper were waiting. As soon as they seen him, they jumped up like their names had been called out for the winning prize at a fate or something.

'I have nothing to say,' he said exiting the car.

'Come on,' the female reporter said, carrying a cassette recorder over her shoulder and a mike connected to it in one hand.

The young guy she had in toe was snapping away like every shot was his last.

Williams was about to repeat what he had already told them when she cut him off.

'The information I have, said there was something strange happening at that farm, and its good information,' she said thrusting the mike into his face.

Williams knew she had her sources, he had gotten some good stuff from her in the past, he also knew there was no way he could indulge in her suspicions.

'You're paying a lot of money for gossip,' he told her as he walked away, heading for the side entrance.

'Twenty-four-hours,' she shouted, pressing the stop button on the recorder.

Williams knew what that meant. Plenty of times in the past, when he had needed a favour, he had been given the same amount of time. He allowed the door to close behind him, shutting them out. But the reality was, the clock was ticking before whatever they were going to run would hit the morning paper stands, then the real circus would begin, especially if it was quiet on other news fronts.

Williams made his way passed the custody desk.

'Robert,' came the familiar voice from the custody sergeant.

Williams stopped and turned.

'Yes,' he said, looking at him.

'I need you to go and visit a lady up at Morton farm.'

'Why?'

'She thinks there has been someone snooping around.'

'Send a couple of bobbies then.'

'I have, but she is threatening to go to the papers if she doesn't get a senior detective.'

'I'll send Jackson then.'

'No can do, remember all that trouble last year with the farm equipment going missing.'

'Yes.'

'Well, she's the one that had us for toast with the press, remember?'

Williams didn't need reminding. It made the nationals, and to say there was hell to pay wouldn't come close, not after she had informed them that she had told the police about strangers snooping around.

'Give me the address, I'll pop over this evening,' he said shaking his head.

The desk sergeant handed over a piece of paper. Williams took it and stuffed it in his back pocket, not bothering to look what was on it, he had more pressing things on his mind.

'And by the way, you're wanted on the second floor.'

Williams didn't look back. He climbed the two flights of stairs and stopped at the super's door. He knocked and waited. The voice was clear as he was instructed to enter. The super stretched out his arm, instructing Williams to sit. Williams knew it wasn't going to be a quick chat, and how much info had he been given by Jackson, about Donna and the professor.

'I have been in contact with the powers that be, and have been informed that for now, you are to continue with the investigation.'

'How is the commissioner.'

'It goes higher than that.'

'Wow, Home secretary.

The super shook his head. Williams could only think of the PM that was above the home secretary, but why would these murders need to go that far up the chain, unless they knew something he didn't.

'Anyway, that's my problem,' the super said, looking at him, waiting for some information.

Williams explained he had sent Jackson back to question everyone again and informed him of the possible sighting of a car in the vicinity at the time. He neglected to tell him of the professor and Donna. If Jackson had informed him of them, he figured he could pass them off as being in the wrong place at the wrong time, maybe.

Williams decided to give him something else to worry about.

'Sir, the local paper has told me we have twenty-four-hours before they run with the story. Williams figured it would keep him busy and away from Donna and the professor.

'Not good,' he said standing and walking to the window.

'My thoughts exactly sir.'

'It will be like a bloody circus down there, what do they know?'

'Well, she told me she had some good info.'

'And do you believe her?'

'Knowing her as I do, I would say yes.'

The super turned and sat down.

'It's only a matter of time sir before it breaks,' Williams told him.

'I'm going to need to make some calls, we need to keep a lid on this.'

Williams could see him thinking. If he played it well, he would be onwards and upwards to better things. But likewise, if it fell apart, he would need a fall guy, and Williams knew he would be in the firing line.

CHAPTER 22

Wiry fingers grasped the side of the door and slid it across the floor, exposing the stranger. He pulled himself up from the hole that had kept him hidden from prying eyes for decades. The wooden stairs creaked as he made his way from the basement. Particles of dust rose into the air with every step, leaving an impression of his size twelve boots.

The stranger looked out of the kitchen window. Rain was streaming down, and the night would give him cover for what he had in mind. He watched as two rats scurried across the back yard, being eyed by a feral cat that was taking cover in a recessed window to an outhouse on the right of the farmhouse.

The stranger knew how the cat felt. The excitement of the chase, the anticipation as you got closer to your pray. The cat didn't move as it watched the two rats disappear down a hole under the outhouse. The stranger knew the cat wasn't in a hurry. The rats would need to exit the hole again and the cat had all the time in the world. But that wasn't something the stranger had. He needed to quench the fire that was burning inside.

He made his way from the house to the barn, pulling the double doors open with ease. There stood the car that had taken him to the site of his previous feast, but that was a couple of days ago and the burning was rising.

The stranger pulled onto the main road, heading for his next fill. The closer he got the more excited he became. He slowed and pulled from the road into a lay-by, he didn't want to get too close without first checking all was quiet. A five-minute walk to the dirt track that led to his prise was blocked by a mettle gate that he easily vaulted. He trudged up the track, scanning the area for anything that didn't fit. He stopped, standing next to the tall hedge he had followed to the front of the secluded farmhouse.

All looked quiet, except for a sliver of light that was showing from a downstairs window. The stranger took one last look, just to be sure, before crossing the track and stopping in front of the house.

Two knocks penetrated the silence as he stood waiting, rain droplets falling from the ends of his jet-black hair. The windows in the door showed light that had filled the hallway as a door was opened, allowing the light to escape. The door opened in front of him. Standing there was the figure of an old lady slightly stooped forward with age.

'Yes?' she said, her voice croaky.

The stranger couldn't believe how easy it was to get people to open their doors to complete strangers. Maybe it was a false sense of security or was it they didn't want to be rude. Who knows, but they were fools he figured.

He used the same tactic as his previous visits. If it works why change he figured. Right enough he was allowed entry without any hesitation. The stranger closed the door behind himself and followed her down the small corridor to the room on the right.

He watched as she made her way to a low chair that had been placed next to an open fire that was crackling away. A TV was situated to the right of the fireplace and a two-seater sofa sat directly in front of the fire. The room looked warm and cosy, with pictures of what he presumed were her family. A black and white photo sat on a table next to her chair of what he presumed was her wedding photo.

She eased herself down to the chair dropping the last couple of inches or so, with a sigh. The expenditure of energy had taken its toll. She removed the phone from the table and offered it to him. He took the phone from her and placed it back on the table, leaning over her. She had a confused look on her face. The stranger stood looking down at her, a broad smile across his face.

She watched in horror as the stranger she had invited into her home started to transform in front of her very eyes.

'No,' she said trying to push him away, but it was futile. The stranger turned her head to the side exposing the rich source of nectar coursing through her veins. Slowly he could feel the burning he had been craving start to dissipate as the life-giving blood for him was slowly draining from her.

He staggered to the fireplace, knocking pictures and ornaments to the floor with blood dripping from his chin and his legs weak. He knew it would only be temporary before the effects wore off and the sweet taste of blood would give him that elation he was craving. He looked down at the dried-up corpse of the old lady that had happily let him enter. He felt nothing for her. No more so than the cat that would kill and eat the rat it was pursuing.

The stranger closed the door on his way out. He felt elated once again, leaping down the track and clearing the gate in one leap. He walked the rest of the way to the car, just in case any motorists drove by. He drove back and parked the car and closed the doors to the barn. He sat in silence watching the cat that was still waiting and watching from the windowsill. He had nowhere to be and later that evening he would no doubt witness another one of life's struggles take place.

CHAPTER 23

Williams left the station, thankfully the reporter and her sidekick had gone, but he knew it was only going to get worse. Once they had a story, they were like dogs with a bone, but at least for now he could drive away without all the constant questioning.

He made his way over to the hotel, maybe they would have had a quieter afternoon than the morning. He parked at the front and made his way up the steps. He allowed the revolving door to continue spinning as he stepped into the foyer. He was about to head for the reception when he spotted them sitting at one of the tables to his right.

'We have been waiting for you,' the professor said as Williams approached.

'I told you; I don't keep regular hours.'

'We have ordered a table for the three of us, thought you would enjoy a proper meal,' the professor told him, using his stick to help him stand.

'I still haven't finished yet,' Williams said.

'Surely you are entitled to an hour,' donna said looking at him.

Williams hadn't eaten a proper meal in days, maybe even longer, everything seemed to be consumed on the go.

'Why not,' he said, thinking he only had a basic call that should be delt with by uniform.

The three walked across to the restaurant where a lady was waiting as they entered.

'Miss wade, table for three,' Donna said to the woman that was looking at them from behind a small podium. She looked down at the book she had in front of her and then back at donna.

'Table three,' she said stepping out.

'It's ok, we can find it,' donna said, stopping the woman in her tracks.

The three headed to the far end, stopping at the last but one table. Williams could feel the bounce in the plush green flowery carpet beneath his feet. The table was set for four places, standard he thought. Donna sat facing the two men looking back the way they had come.

Black leather-bound menus with gold writing of the name of the hotel were already placed on the table. Williams ordered the full roast; it had been a long time since he had eaten one. The fact it was the middle of the week didn't stop him. The professor did the same, but donna ordered the chicken salad, and the professor ordered a bottle of wine for them.

'We found out some information this afternoon,' the professor told him.

Williams wondered how long it would take before the conversation resorted to why they were there.

'And how did you come by it?' Williams asked, with a slightly annoyed look on his face.

'We popped into the local pub and got talking to a couple of locals.'

Donna nodded, confirming he was telling the truth.

Williams was about to say something when he stopped due to a young man standing at the table with the bottle of wine the professor had ordered. They waited until Donnas and the professor's glass had been filled, Williams refused, he was still on duty and had one more call to make.

Once the waiter had gone Williams continued.

'So, what did you find out then?'

'Well, it seems that some years back, similar things had taken place.'

'How long back?'

'He didn't say, just that people from London came and removed the bodies.'

'And who said this?'

'Didn't catch his name, you donna.'

She shook her head, 'his friend that was with him said there had been livestock issues too,' backing up the professor.

Williams thought about what they had said. Maybe they were telling the truth with what his super had told him that afternoon.

'I was informed I could stay on the case for now,' Williams told them.

Donna looked at him with a puzzled look.

'But if they take you off it, who will replace you?' she asked.

'I thought you were the senior detective,' the professor chipped in with.

'I am.'

'Then how can they remove you from the case.'

Williams shrugged his shoulders.

'I'm not a conspiracy sort of person, but I do think there is more to this case than the powers that be are letting on,' the professor said taking a sip of wine.

Williams didn't want to admit it, but the professor was probably right.

Their meals were brought and the three tucked in. It was a real treat for Williams to be sitting down eating a good tasty meal, instead of the usual canteen stuff or a sandwich on the go.

They waited until they had all finished before resuming the topic of conversation.

No sooner than Donna had placed the knife and fork down, than the professor had a question.

'If you get removed from the case, does that mean, we are all removed?'

Williams could see the two of them staring at him. He waited a few seconds before answering.

'No.'

He could see the relief on the professor's face, not so much for Donna.

'I'm the lead detective, and no suit from London is going to take over.'

'Good man,' the professor said tapping him on the back.

Williams removed his coat from the back of the chair.

'Going so soon?' the professor asked.

'Need to make a house call.'

Williams removed his wallet from his inside pocket.

'Please, it's my treat,' the professor said holding his hand up in the stop sign sort of way.

'Are you sure?'

'Wouldn't have it any other way,' the professor told him.

'Thank you.'

'My pleasure.'

Williams walked out of the hotel, thinking about what they had said. With what the super had told him and how far up the chain of command it went, they were probably telling the truth. But that was for another day. Right now, he had a house call to make.

CHAPTER 24

Williams stopped at the gate that led to the cottage. The gate was stiff and rusty, and hard to open. He returned to the car and stopped just past the gate to close it. unfortunately, he hadn't spotted one of the dips in the track that had filled with water and stepped straight into it, the water over filled his shoe and soaked his foot. The puddle had just made his mood worse, as he couldn't see why he needed to make a personal call, just because she had the number to the local papers.

He continued up the track and parked next to the house. He exited the car and knocked, at least he would be out of the rain once she opened. There was no movement, so he knocked harder. He could see light coming from a room halfway down the hallway. He made his way to the window, but the curtains were closed. He knocked on the window and called out telling the occupier he was the police, still nothing. He made his way to the gate at the side of the property, luckily it opened, he didn't fancy the climb. The rear was locked up and in darkness. He tried knocking the back door, but still nothing. He made his way back to the front of the house and stood back, looking the property over, rain bouncing off his face.

One last time he thought. He banged on the front door hard, if they were there then they would surely hear that. He waited but still got no response. He had a choice to make, does he come back tomorrow or force entry, he needed a reason for the latter. He returned to the car and stopped at the rear, removing the wheel brace. The small window that was nearest the lock shattered with ease. He dropped the brace to the floor and opened the door. The excuse he was going to use was he thought she may have had a fall and was in need of assistance, it's all he could think of, and he didn't fancy returning tomorrow.

'Hello,' he shouted as he stepped into the hallway. He made his way to the room that was illuminating the hallway. The door was half closed so he pushed it open slowly, he didn't want to startle her any more than necessary. What he hadn't expected was the sight that greeted him.

He stepped to the rear of the two-seater and looked at the prune like corpse. He needed to call it in. He knew this second incident changed things, probably removing him from the case. He backed tracked out of the house and drove back down the track, stopping to open the gate. He didn't stop to close it, he had more pressing things on his mind. He was one-hundred percent certain now that everything the professor had told him was true.

He parked outside and went in, not stopping at the reception. He knocked the door and waited.

Donna looked at him with a surprised look on her face.

'You and the professor need to come with me.'

'Why?' she asked.

'I'll explain on the way,' he told her, water still dripping from his hair.

'You will need to give me time to change,' she said, holding the white bath robe closed.

'What room is the professor in?'

'Next door,' she said pointing to the left.

Williams walked away, hearing the door close.

The professor was still dressed, except his waistcoat was half undone.

'Detective, what a surprise to see you again this evening, he said, looking at Williams. What have you been doing,' he said noticing his sodden hair.

'I need you and donna to come with me,' Williams told him.

'Whatever for at this time of night?' he said with a puzzled look.

'Just get your coat, you need to see this,' Williams told him.

The professor retrieved his coat and stick and stepped out into the hallway. Donna followed and the three made their way to his car.

'Your car is certainly more comfortable than ours,' the professor said, getting comfortable.

Williams didn't answer, the car wasn't something he was thinking about. He knew what he was doing was risky. If he got caught with them in toe, he knew he was in big trouble, but he also knew that once he radioed it in, then there was a good chance the case would be buried.

'Where are we going?' donna asked from the back seat.

Williams didn't want to tell them, he figured the professor would be elated, but donna would probably not want to go in, and more importantly he needed witnesses.

'Were nearly there,' he told her, seeing her face flash now and again as they passed the streetlamps.

'I think it's rather exciting,' the professor said, watching the windscreen wipers throwing the rain off the side of the car.

Williams slowed and turned in, bouncing them up the track.

The three stepped out into the pouring rain. Williams stopped at the front door and waited for them to join him.

'Well, who broke the window?' the professor said, as he watched Williams put his arm in and open the door.

'I did,' Williams said, stepping into the hallway.

'I thought you were supposed to stop crime,' Donna said, following the two into the house.

Williams didn't answer, once they were in the Livingroom, who broke the window wouldn't matter.

'What your about to see, can't be spoken about to anyone,' Williams said stopping at the door.

'Of cause,' the professor said.

Williams knew he would have said anything to get into that room, but he had brought them hear knowing the possibility of what could go wrong. Williams stepped in and to the side. The professor followed and stood next to him staring at the corpse. Donna took a quick look and turned away.

'Why did you do that?' she asked.

'Because once I report this, the case will be taken over and I need witnesses to what's taken place,' Williams told her.

The professor walked around the sofa and stopped in front of the corpse. Williams watched as the professor looked closely, followed by looking at the fallen photos that had landed on the floor before turning to Williams.

'It seems there has been a struggle,' the professor told him.

'No,' Williams said joining him in front of the fireplace.

'How not,' the professor said pointing to the broken photos.

'If you look closely, the spatters of blood are beneath the photos, indicating the photos fell after the, Williams looked at the corpse, this, he said gesturing to the corpse.

The professor had another look.

'Yes, I see what you mean, the blood would be on top of the photos,' the professor said looking more intently.

The three heard a noise from the kitchen. They all stood bolt upright, looking at the door. Donna joined them at the fireplace, looking at the two of them. Williams walked to the door and waited, nothing. He poked his head out looking up and down the hallway and up the stairs that were in front of him. The two had joined him and were peeking out. The kitchen door opened slightly, Donna grabbed Williams by the arm, if he was still hear, what would they do. She knew they were no match, not even close, and probably would end up like the old lady.

A scruffy looking tabby stepped out from behind the door, meowing as it made its way to them.

'We need to go,' Donna said.

Williams knew what she was driving at, and she was right. It's something he hadn't really thought about, until now.

'I'll drop you back and call it in,' he told them, closing the front door behind them.

Williams knew tomorrow things were going to change, but by how much he wasn't sure.

CHAPTER 25

Williams had dropped Donna and the professor back and was waiting at the gate leading to the cottage track. He didn't fancy waiting alone, just in case. Headlights shone in the rear-view-mirror, bobbing up and down following the contour of the road, slowly getting closer. Jackson stopped next to him and wound the window down.

'What's going on sir,' Jackson said, trying to peer over the top of Williams's car.

'We got another one,' Williams told him.

A flashing blue light appeared in the distance. Williams waited until they got close enough before driving up the track, with Jackson following. They may not know what they could be heading into, but he did, and he wanted safety in numbers.

Williams stopped at the front door, followed by Jackson, then the squad car with two officers in.

'Jackson, you come with me, you two, stay here,' he told the two officers.

The two did as they were ordered and stood as close to the hallway as they could, trying to get out of the driving rain. Williams stepped back into the room for the third time that evening.

'Sir what's going on?' Jackson asked again, standing next to him with his long green coat dripping with water.

'I have no idea,' Williams said, knowing full well he did.

'Maybe the doc can tell us,' Williams told him.

Williams could hear talking at the front, he stepped out just in time to see the doc passing the two constables.

'I take it the window was how he gained entry,' the doc said standing in front of him.

'No, that was me,' Williams said.

The doc looked over the top of his spectacles at him.

'I needed to gain entry.'

The doc shrugged his shoulders as if to say not his problem, or concern.

'In there,' Williams said standing to the side.

The doc walked in and placed his bag down at the side of the chair. He looked the corpse over before putting on some gloves. He immediately took a closer look at the neck before standing upright.

'It seems we have the same modus-operandi,' he said as he removed the gloves.

Williams could hear more voices from the front. He knew how most of the bobbies in the local area would descend on the place if allowed.

'Go and send one of them down to the gate and stop anyone else from coming up, unless they are needed, and then check the rest of the house,' he told Jackson.

Jackson did as he was ordered. Williams waited until Jackson was out of the way before speaking to the doc.

'Look, with this new murder, the case is going to be taken over, and we are going to be side lined.'

By whom?' the doc asked looking annoyed.

'Powers that be, I need you to get as much evidence as you can, and I want you to do two copies of everything, this one, and the last ones,' Williams told him.

'Hold on a minute.'

'Look, after tomorrow, all this is going to disappear, and I don't like the fact that that family and this old lady won't mean a thing to them.'

'Who's going to close it down?'

'Not sure, but you have to trust me.'

The two were interrupted by the arrival of the photographer.

Williams nodded to the doc, implying for him to follow. The two left the Livingroom and entered the kitchen.

'I need you to do the autopsy tonight.'

'Why?'

'Because.'

'But I have people coming tomorrow from London to take a look.'

'Tomorrow will be too late, as soon as I inform the super, he will be on the phone.'

'To whom?' he asked again.

'We'll find out tomorrow.'

The doc didn't say anything. He retrieved his bag from the Livingroom and made his way out.

'The rest of the house is all clear sir,' Jackson said descending the stairs.

'Sir, what's going on with these bodies,' Jackson repeated.

'I wish I knew,' Williams lied to him again.

'I need you to make sure that when the van gets here, she is taken straight to the morgue, the doc will be waiting,' and keep everyone outside you understand.'

'Where you going sir?'

'Back to the station.'

Williams knew he needed to collect something, especially after his conversation with the doctor.

CHAPTER 26

Williams entered via the rear, the place where prisoners were brought in, out of the way from prying eyes.

'I hear we have another one,' the desk sergeant said on seeing him enter.

Williams nodded.

'You need to inform him,' he said, pointing his finger up.

'Tell him in the morning, it ain't going to change what's happened if he knows now or not.'

Williams knew it would change everything, but he needed time to complete what he had to do.

'Robert! he want's informing straight away if there were any new developments.'

'It's 23:30, what's he going to do at this time.'

The desk sergeant raised an eyebrow before turning away. Williams knew he could trust him not to inform the super, not tonight anyway. But he would inform him of the new developments in the morning and by then Williams would have what he wanted.

The second floor was in darkness, just like he thought it would be. He stopped at the super's door and turned the handle, the door opened and he entered, closing the door behind himself. Some light from outside gave him a little illumination, but not much. The metal filing cabinets were the first place he looked. He closed the top draw and continued working his way down. He closed the bottom draw and stood up, looking at the desk. He slid the chair out and sat, pulling himself to the desk. He looked at the draws, if he had locked them, then what he wanted would be out of reach. He pulled on the first draw; it slid out smoothly, and there it was, just sitting there. He removed the file of the first murders and closed the draw and pushed the chair back.

He made his way back down the stairs and passed the custody desk, the sergeant nodded but took no notice of the file he was holding, why would he, he had seen Williams come and go thousands of times with files.

Williams placed the file on the passenger seat and drove to the morgue, he knew he had to have the file back before the super arrived in the morning.

He knocked the door and waited. Sure enough, the doc opened it.

'Thanks for this,' Williams said, following him in.

'You're just in time to help,' the doc said, leading Williams down the corridor.

His way off payback, Doctors, a strange breed he thought.

The two pushed through the double doors. The fresh corpse from that evening had been delivered and placed on the metal table. The bright lights were in stark contrast to outside and Williams could hear the doc pulling on his rubber gloves. Williams stood to the left, looking down at her dried up remains.

'Shell we get started,' the doc said sliding a small metal table next to him with an array of utensils on. Williams thought it looked more like a carpenter's tool kit than something you would see in a hospital, but then again, it wasn't part of the hospital people would get to see.

Williams watched as the doc turned the head to the side and examined the neck. Williams listened as the dried-up skin cracked and opened. The doc removed a scalpel and proceeded to make a long cut down the chest.

'I need a cigarette,' Williams said, leaving him to continue on his own.

Williams stepped outside, wedging the door open, using the fire extinguisher. Knowing what happened in an autopsy and watching one was two different things, not something he wanted to witness. He finished his cigarette and returned, hoping it was completed.

The corpse was covered with a white sheet as he stepped in, thankfully it was concluded.

'Cause of death was the same as the family,' the doc said as Williams entered his office.

'Did you think about what I said earlier?' Williams asked.

'Can't do it, sorry, however, there are some blank forms, the doc nodded to a set of trays sitting on a filing cabinet, 'I mean if you want to copy them yourself, that's up to you.'

Williams knew he was covering his back, and why not, it wasn't his problem. He removed some of the forms and placed them in the file the doc had handed to him.

'Thanks for this,' Williams said, holding up the file.

The doc nodded and turned back to his desk. Williams took the hint, the doc wasn't going to inform on him, but he also wasn't going to get involved.

Williams headed home; his night was far from finished. He spent the next hour copying the forms word for word. He retrieved his camera and loaded a new film. The photos were placed on his dining table, his problem was he wouldn't know what the quality was like until the film was developed, and he needed someone that wouldn't ask too many questions.

He headed back to the station. The desk sergeant was booking in a couple of guys caught trying to break into a local off-licence. Williams walked past and headed upstairs. He placed the file back and closed the door, he had what he needed. He looked at the clock 03:15, he knew later that day things were going to change.

CHAPTER 27

The beep from the alarm woke Williams. He leaned over and pressed the snooze button and climbed back into bed, curling up under the sheets, what he wanted to do was turn the alarm off and go back to sleep. It was 04:00 before he had finished and climbed into bed. The three hours sleep had done nothing for the fatigue he felt.

He lay there curled up, warm and comfortable, barely able to open his eyes, thinking of the day ahead. The alarm started beeping again, he knew he couldn't hit the snooze button, he needed to be there when the super arrived.

He dressed and stepped outside. Thick fog had settled on everything it had touched. Half the street in both directions was hidden behind the cloak that had replaced the heavy rain. Williams reversed from his drive and started the slow drive in, not like he was in a hurry, he had a good idea what was coming, especially if what the professor had said was true after his meeting in the pub. But who would be taking over, what department would seal and bury the case. But that was for later, as far as he was concerned, it was business as usual. He would inform the super and then pull the troops in to start the usual door to door, any information he could gather now, would help with his own investigation. Just because someone wanted it shut down, didn't mean it would be, unofficially of cause.

Williams slowed and stopped outside the rear, he had seen no reporters, maybe they had already decided to run with what they had, that wasn't his problem, so why worry about something you have no control over.

Williams opened the door to see the desk sergeant sitting there.

'Didn't expect you in this early,' he said looking at him.

Williams didn't respond, just pointed his finger in the air.

The desk sergeant nodded, knowing exactly what he meant.

Inform me as soon as he arrives Williams told him and continued to his office. He closed the door and sat at his desk. A couple of detectives were already in, but he was too tired to talk to them. Jackson followed him in, re-closing the door. Williams knew how he felt, he looked the worse for wear too from the lack of sleep. Williams watched as he placed his coat on the coat rack and slumped in his chair.

'Busy day today,' Williams said looking at him.

'Yes sir,' he said, his eyes only half open.

William's phone rang. He picked it up, listened and placed it back without saying anything. Here goes he thought, leaving Jackson and closing the door.

The super nodded to the empty chairs in front of his desk. Williams sat and waited until the super had finished hanging his coat before sitting opposite him.

'Sir there was another one last night.'

'You mean the same as the family.'

'Afraid so, exact time is pretty much impossible to tell, due to the state of the body, but we know she rang the station in the afternoon, so we have a window of about eight hours.'

'Who found her?'

'I did, I went to make the house call.'

Williams passed the file from the doc and sat waiting. The super quickly flicked through and placed it in the top draw of his desk with the previous one that Williams had replaced. He was about to tell him he was going to get the troops together and start the door to door, but decided against it, he wasn't sure if he would be told to hold fire until he had made his call.

'Leave it with me,' the super told nim.

'Sir.'

Williams stood, leaving him flicking through his card holder he had placed in front of himself.

'Jackson, I want you and as many bodies you can muster and go door to door, I want to know if there was anything out of the ordinary at least one week before last night.'

'It's pretty isolated up their sir.'

'I know, that's why I want you to widen the search.'

Williams retrieved a map from his desk and opened it, placing it down he found the location and showed Jackson an outline of where he wanted him to work.

'But that will take most of the day.'

'Best get started then,' Williams told him.

Jackson took a deep breath, showing he wasn't happy with his new assignment. Williams knew time was against him, and Jacksons discomfort was part of the job, he had been on plenty of door knocking when he was a sergeant.

'And by the way, you are to report directly to me,' you understand.

Jackson nodded before closing the door and heading into the operations room. Williams watched as Jackson and four detectives left. He held the phone to his ear and dialled the number. The phone was answered on the second ring.

'Can you put me through to room forty-eight, no please or thank you.'

Williams waited as the phone rang out, judging by the time it took he figured she wasn't up and about yet.

'Hello,' came the groggy voice of Donna.

'Good, you're up.'

'I am now.'

'Listen, I will meet you and the professor in the café at ten.'

'Ok,' she said, in a sleepy voice.

He placed the phone down and removed his coat from the stand. He had a call to make, and he knew just the man he needed.

CHAPTER 28

Williams stepped outside and climbed in his car, still no reporters present, he figured they were going to run with what they had. The fog he had drove through to get there was still like pea soup. He slowed and turned off the main road, a narrow lane with tall un-kept hedges on both sides concealed the house he was looking for. He had busted the owner before, for counterfeiting, that's how he knew he wouldn't ask too many questions.

Slowly the house started to appear out of the gloom, first an outline, then the closer he got the more detail started to show. It didn't look much from the front, but Williams knew that in the past, the interior had been turned into a lucrative operation. He would turn a blind eye if he produced the goods he had come for.

Williams stopped and walked down the path, well what was left of it, weeds had grown through the joints and lifted some of the pathing. The fence that would have separated the garden was missing, except for a couple of stumps sticking out of the ground. The door needed a good paint and the windows on either side were blacked out. Williams knocked and waited; he knew he didn't keep regular hours. A dog started barking, the deep bark told him it was a big one.

The door was opened and the tall thin frame with long unkept hair stood in front of him. The puzzled look told Williams he had no idea what he was there for.

'You going to let me in then Steven?' Williams said.

'I ain't got nothing to hide,' he replied, his teeth stained from nicotine.

'Glad to hear it, I need a favour,' Williams told him.

The comment changed his demeaner. His head lifted a little as if to say what you want something from me. Williams was allowed to enter.

'I hope the dog's away.'

'He's in the kitchen.'

Williams followed him down the hallway and through the first door on the left. The room was square and a green couch that had gone thread bear sat in front of an open fire. The chimney breast had gone black from soot and a bucket of coal sat to the left, but the fire had died over night and the room was cold.

'So, what do you want from me?' he asked standing there in black faded sports bottoms and creased grey jumper.

'I need you to develop this for me,' Williams said, retrieving the film from his pocket and holding it in front of himself.

'What's on it?' he asked looking at the canister.

'Nothing important.'

'Then why don't you get one of your guys to do it?'

Williams knew he was asking all the right questions; he was slowly backing him into a corner.

'There's a back log and I need them now.'

Steven didn't answer, he just stood, looking at the canister.

'It's from an active case, and what's on there can't be talked about to anyone, you understand.'

He nodded his head and instructed Williams to follow. The two left the living room and headed upstairs. Bare floorboards and wallpaper that was coming from the walls ran up the stairs and continued along the hallway. Williams followed him to the door at the far end. The two stepped inside. To the left a table stood holding white trays filled with liquid that had been placed next to each other. On the right, shelving held what Williams figured were the chemicals that was needed to develop the film.

Steven held out his hand.

'What's in it for me?' he asked.

'One, I don't come and raid this place anytime soon, and two, ten quid for your time.'

Williams gave him a dead stair.

'Ok,' he said taking the film.'

A done deal Williams thought. Steven probably thought he would have something over him if he needed it, but Williams knew it was totally deniable from his point of view. Steven removed a small canister from the shelving and a pair of scissors and put on a pair of rubber gloves. Williams didn't interfere, he watched as he pulled some of the film out and cut it.

'You need to turn the light off,' steven told him holding the film.

Williams knew that it needed to be in darkness, so he obliged. The room was completely blacked out, not even a sliver of light from under the door. A few minutes passed when steven told him he could turn the lights back on, it took a few seconds for his eyes to adjust.

'That's it?' Williams asked.

'No, I needed to get it into the developing tank first.'

Williams watched as he removed some bottles from the bottom shelf and took them to a sink at the far end and placed them in a bowl and started to run the hot tap.

'They need to be warmed up,' he told Williams.

Williams had no idea what was going on, but it did look interesting, he watched as he placed a thermometer in the bottles.

'That will do,' he said removing one of the bottles and turning off the tap.

Steven poured some of the liquid into the canister that held the film.

'That's the developer I just poured in,' he told Williams.

Williams didn't say anything, he just watched as he agitated the film every now and again. He watched as steven kept his eye on the clock that he had sitting next to the sink. The developer was poured back into its original bottle and another bottle was removed from the bowl and poured in.

'You don't want to get too close, this stuff is very toxic,' he said.

Williams took a step back, he seemed to know what he was doing. He watched as he agitated the film at arm's length.

'This stuff will burn your skin bad,' he said not taking his eye from the canister.

It had been over five minutes when steven poured the chemical back into its bottle. He retrieved the canister and took it back to the sink and started to use the water from the bowl to wash the film. The third bottle that hadn't been warmed like the first two was poured in. A couple of minutes later the chemical was poured back into its bottle and steven held the canister in front of himself.

Time to see if it's worked, he said removing the top. A white roll that the film had been wound around was withdrawn. Steven held it up to the light, unrolling the film slowly. Williams joined him, looking over his shoulder at the images.

'Good, we need to leave it to dry out.'

'How long,' Williams asked.

'About an hour.'

Williams watched as he hung the developed film from a wire over the sink.

'You can come back later if you want,' he told him.

'I'll wait.'

Williams wasn't going to let the film out of his site, just in case he made a duplicate, it would give him wiggle room in the future.

'Please yourself.'

The two headed downstairs. Williams looked at his watch, it was already 09:00 and his meeting at the café was for 10:00, he would be late, but keeping the film safe was his first priority.

CHAPTER 29

The hour had gone slowly. The dog had been put outside, not at Williams request, but judging by the way it had been jumping up the window, Williams was grateful, he didn't fancy going toe to toe with a German shepherd, especially one that had that level of energy.

Williams followed Steven back upstairs. Steven retrieved the film and took it over to a machine on the shelving. He cut the first negative from the film and placed it in the top of the machine. A blank white paper was placed underneath and steven flicked a switch. The image from the negative appeared on the paper. Williams watched as he turned a dial at the side, sharpening the image.

'That should do it,' he said, looking at it.

He flicked the switch and changed the blank paper before turning the machine back on. Williams watched as he kept an eye on the clock.

He removed the paper and turned to the first of the trays. He placed the blank paper in and used a pair of tongs to submerge it under the liquid. Slowly an image started to appear. About a minute later and the image was clearly visible. Steven removed it and repeated the prosses with the next two trays. He held the photo, allowing the liquid to drain, looking at the image.

'Is that a body?' he asked.

Williams looked at the photo. It showed the image of the farmer's body from the barn.

'Like I said, it's something that you can't talk about, you understand?'

'Yer, I know, you said.'

'How long before the rest are done?'

'Hour or so.'

'Good, get on with it then.'

Williams waited, collecting the negatives in turn, one by one. He wasn't going to leave anything to chance, he didn't trust him, he knew the first chance he had, he would sell them to the highest bidder, probably the papers. Williams hadn't expected it to take as long as it had, but if he was going to stay on the case then he needed all the proof he could get. Williams removed a brown envelope that he had folded in half from his inside pocket and placed the photos in.

'So, what you going to do with them?' Steven asked.

That was a good question, he wasn't too sure himself, didn't really know how it could help the case, maybe leverage if top brass found out about his private investigation.

'Thanks for this,' Williams said, ignoring the question and removing his wallet and opening it. Steven seen his warrant card as he flipped the wallet open.

'What we agreed upon,' Williams said, handing over the ten pounds.

There was no hesitation, he folded the cash and kept hold of it in his fist. Williams turned and made his way outside. The fog hadn't eased, and he was running late, he had arranged to meet them at 10:00, but it was closer to 11:30. He reversed and headed back to the hotel, no need to try the café he thought, he wouldn't have waited around that length of time, so why would they.

He stopped outside of the hotel and walked up to the reception. The gentleman that had spoken to him previously and was a little annoyed that he hadn't been in the loop was waiting as he approached.

'I would like to speak to miss wade.'

'You are sir?' he asked.

He knew who he was from their last encounter, maybe still a little annoyed.

'Detective chief inspector Williams,' he said, with a stern look.

'There has been a message left for you sir.'

He turned and removed a piece of paper from the rear shelving.

Williams took the note and turned away.

Need to find some information.
see you at seven in the restaurant.
Donna.

What are they up to he thought. He didn't like the idea that they were off on their own, up to all sorts. They had already been pulled once, the next time they wouldn't be so lucky, not if Jackson collared them. He just had to hope for the best.

He pushed the note in his pocket and headed back to the car. It was lunch time, and his stomach was rumbling, but he needed to get back to the station, Jackson should be back by now and he needed the information, that's if they had gathered any, judging by the first one it was highly unlikely.

He started the car and drove back slowly, the fog getting thicker by the hour, and by this rate it would be walking speed at best. He stopped at the side of the station, still no reporters. He was sure that only meant one thing, they were running with what they had. He used the front entrance and walked up the stairs. The hustle and bustle and noise from people working and talking was missing as he pushed through the double doors to the incident room. Williams looked around; everyone were sitting at their desks with their heads buried in paperwork. Williams hadn't seen it before. He opened the door to his office; Jackson was sitting at his desk doing the same.

'What's going on?'

'Sir, your wanted upstairs,' Jackson said raising his head.

'Ok, I will go up in a minute.'

'Sir, there are some people hear.'

'Who?'

'I think they are from the government.'

'Why do you think that?' Williams asked hanging his coat and scarf on the wooden hanger.

'When we got back, the super had come down to meet them personally and escorted them upstairs.'

'You said them, how many?'

'Three. Looked like one was in charge, he walked side by side with the super and the other two followed behind, two of them have taken over the room at the far end,' Jackson nodded to the far end of the incident room.

Williams looked down before turning back to Jackson.

'First things first, did you get any info.'

'Nothing tangible, except a Mrs... Jackson removed his notebook from his draw and opened it, flicking the pages until he got to the one he wanted.

'Yes, a Mrs Selby was coming back from her church Meeting, and she thinks she remembers a car parked just past the entrance to the cottage.

'Colour, make?'

'No, it was raining heavy, and the windows had misted over.'

Williams hadn't expected anything, but it was worth a shot. He left the office and climbed the stairs, he knew who had come was probably a big cheese, that's why the super had come down to meet him. But Williams knew he oversaw the case, and they would need a good reason to remove him. Time to find out who they are, he thought, as he knocked the super's door.

CHAPTER 30

Williams opened the door and entered. The super was sitting at his desk and a man in a dark grey suit sat opposite. The two looked at him as he closed the door.

'You wanted to see me sir?' Williams said.

'Yes, sit down.'

Williams did as instructed, he knew why he was there, but he wasn't going to make it easy for them.

'This is captain Andrews from the ministry of defence.'

Williams held out his hand. Andrews obliged and nodded politely.

Williams waited to see who spoke first.

'As you are aware, this case has some peculiar characteristics about it, and after speaking to some people, they thought it would be better to turn the case over to some specialist,' the super said looking at Williams.

'What people?' Williams asked, looking at them and waiting to see what they would come up with.

There was an awkward silence.

'People that you don't need to know about,' Andrews said.

'I agree about the case, but why can't we work together?' Williams asked.

The question seemed to throw them a little.

'It's already been decided,' the super said.

'So why the MOD,' Williams asked looking at the super.

It was Andrews that answered.

'We believe that someone is injecting the victims with chemicals as to dry the bodies out, so you see it comes under our jurisdiction.'

Williams watched as Andrews nodded to the super. He knew it was complete garbage, but he also knew there was nothing he could do about it, but he wasn't going to make it easy for them and walk away like a good little boy.

'So, if someone's using chemical weapons, shouldn't we be involved in the investigation too, after all, its on our patch.'

'Too dangerous,' Andrews said.

'We could make it easier for you, we have local knowledge.'

'No can do I'm afraid,' Andrews answered.

'Yorkshire is a very large area, you're going to need men,' Williams told him.

'We have our own, but thanks for the offer.'

Williams was about to interject but was cut off.

'Robert, it's already been settled,' the super told him.

Williams knew there was no point continuing. The super had only used his first name once before, and that was to end a dispute between himself and a visiting DCI from London.

Williams stood, 'you have all the paperwork from the case, I will pull everyone off then.'

'Thank you,' Andrews said before looking back to the super.

Williams turned and left the two of them, his mind was on what to do next as he made his way down the stairs. He tapped the window causing Jackson to look up. Williams gave him the signal to join him in the incident room. Everyone was still at their desks when he entered. He waited a few seconds until Jackson joined them.

'Listen up, I want everything you have on the farm murders and the cottage, and hand them over to Jackson.'

'What's going on sir?' one of the detectives at the front asked.

'Were officially off the case.'

'Jackson, collect everything and hand it over to them,' Williams said nodding to the room at the rear.'

'And get a chain of custody receipt, lets make sure we do it by the book.'

Williams left them and headed back to his office. He knew he would be taken off the case, but it still felt like a slug in the gut now it had actually happened. He picked up the phone and rang the hotel.

'Can you put me through to room forty-eight please.'

Williams waited.

'I'm sorry sir, but no one is answering, can I take a message.'

'No,' he replied and replaced the receiver.

Not knowing what they were up to gave him that dreaded feeling. Jackson entered the office just as Williams was removing his coat from the stand.

'Going out sir.'

'Yes.'

'Where shell I say you have gone, if they ask.'

'I didn't say.'

CHAPTER 31

It was 18:45, Donna and the professor were sitting at one of the tables opposite reception. They watched as Williams crossed the floor heading for them. He passed the three newcomers that were occupying the next table.

'Order you a drink?' the professor asked.

'Why not,' Williams replied.

'Good man, what will it be?'

'A large whisky I think.'

'That sort of a day?' Donna said.

'How did you guess,' Williams replied as he flopped in the chair next to her.

'So, what's so bad?' she asked.

'Well, I'm officially off the case.'

She placed her hand on his arm and squeezed a little.

'There you go,' the professor said placing the double scotch on the table in front of him. Williams picked it up and downed half of it.

'That sort of a day I see.'

'He's off the case,' donna said, looking at the professor.

'Arr,' the professor said as he re-joined them.

'What can you do,' Williams said as he downed the remaining scotch.

'Slow down my good man,' the professor told him as he picked up his own sherry and took a sip.

Williams placed the empty glass on the knee-high table.

'So, what have you two been up to all day?' Williams asked leaning back in the chair.

'Well, this morning we went to the library.'

Sightseeing then, Williams interrupted.'

'No,' donna said in a way that sounded like she was offended with the comment.

The professor ignored it, he knew he was hurting from being dumped off the case.

'I wanted to confirm something,' the professor continued.

'And?' Williams asked.

'It's as I thought.'

Williams turned his head slightly, very subtle, but enough for the professor to get the message.

'Yes, well that brings us on to our next visit, we had to go to church.'

'What?' Williams asked looking back and forth between the pair.

'It's not what you think,' donna said, seeing his dismay.

We armed ourselves the professor said with a straight face.

Williams was about to say something when a woman from the hotel staff stopped next to them.

'Your table reservation is ready miss wade,' she said with a warm smile. Donna thanked her and the three stood.

'I'll join you in a minute,' Williams told them.

He waited for them to enter the dining room before heading through the door to the left of reception and ordering himself another double scotch at the bar. He made his way to the far end of the restaurant and joined them at the table.

'I was going to order a bottle of wine, but I see you have all-ready ordered,' donna said looking at his glass in hand.

Williams didn't reply, he sat next to the professor and downed half of the drink.

'That's not going to get us too far,' the professor told him.

'Depends on where you're going,' Williams said with a slight smile on his face.

Donna and the professor picked up the menu and glanced at each other.

'So, what did you mean, you have armed yourselves?'

The professor closed the menu and placed it down in front of himself.

'That's why we needed to go to church you see.'

'What, you picked up a cross,' Williams said with a grin.

'No, we picked up some holy water,' donna told him.

Williams's mouth dropped a little before he grinned at them. It was just too much for him, he downed the rest of the scotch in one go.

'Carry on without me, I need another drink,' he said before leaving them at the table.

'What do we do?' donna asked, watching him walk away.

'I guess there's nothing we can do, he's had a ruff day, let's order and see what tomorrow brings.

Williams sat with his third double of the night, he knew he had been rude, and he was going to apologise. It was the first time in his career he had been removed from a case and it didn't sit well with him. He watched as the three newcomers that were sitting at the next table get up and headed for the lifts. He thought he seen one of the two men wearing makeup. The woman was for sure, but maybe it was the drink. Maybe the professor was right when he said it wouldn't help. He sat waiting for them to finish, nursing the scotch. The effects of the drink had relaxed him somewhat, so much so he wished he had stayed and ate with them. It was looking like a late fish and chip supper again.

Donna and the professor exited the restaurant and spotted him sitting at the table on his own.

'I thought you had gone,' donna said sternly.

'Please take a seat,' William's asked politely.

Donna moved in first followed by the professor.

'I'm sorry for laughing at you earlier,' Williams said looking at them.

'Sure its not just the drink saying that?' donna said looking at the empty glass.

I'm sure, and I have been thinking, that's if its ok with you of cause, it's just a suggestion.

The two had a puzzled look on their faces, his attitude had changed.

'Why don't you two stay at mine? we are going to need to work closely together from now on.'

Donna looked a bit taken aback by the request, but the professor on the other hand looked like he could have jumped the table and hugged him.

'I suppose we could,' donna said after witnessing the professor's reaction.

'Good, that's settled then, I will wait here for you.'

'What, right now?' donna asked.

'Why not? unless you have a better idea,' Williams replied.

'No no, give us five minutes and we will be straight down,' the professor said getting out of the low chair.

Donna watched as the professor headed for the lifts, she followed him, listening to the clicking sound coming from his walking stick. She couldn't help but notice that the clicks had gotten a little faster than normal.

CHAPTER 32

Present Day

'Mr Williams, would you like a break?' the taller one of the two asked.

'Maybe I could put the kettle on,' Williams replied looking at the walking stick.

'Please allow us,' the taller one said.

He nodded to his partner. Williams now knew who was in charge. He wasn't too sure as he was the one doing all the talking. He thought it was probably the taller one but couldn't be sure. Sometimes the actual one in charge likes to take a back seat in the beginning, just to see how the conversation develops.

'The file says you have lived here all your life?'

'Yes, it was my parents, been here man and boy.'

'And you had two children of your own?'

'Correct, and grandchildren, but I don't get to see them all that much these days.'

'Live far away?'

'New Zealand is a bit of a trek.'

'How long has it been since you last seen them?'

'They came over for their mother's funeral, two years ago now.'

'I'm sorry,' he said.

Williams noticed he tried to give the look that you get when someone is trying to be sorry for you, but they don't really, he had used the look many times himself.

'I found some biscuits next to the sugar,' the shorter one said as he returned with a tray. He placed the cups and saucers out and poured them all a cup.

'My wife's insistence,' Williams said.'

'Don't really see proper teapots these days,' the taller one said.

Williams used the arms of the chair to pull himself forward slightly to reach the table. He picked up the cup and took a sip before replacing it and sitting back, giving a slight wince before continuing.

CHAPTER 33

Donna slowed and turned on to the drive as instructed from the rear seat. The smell of fish and chips filled the car, making her feel hungry, even though she had just eaten. Williams had left his car at the hotel; due to the three doubles he had consumed.

'Well come on then,' Williams said as he exited the rear, grasping his late supper.

The professor followed, leaving donna to retrieve the cases from the boot. Williams opened the front door and stepped in, turning the hall light on. The professor followed, passing the stairs on the left and noticing the door facing him was the kitchen. He followed Williams through the door on the right. The living room was modern and bright, zigzag wallpaper and matching carpet and long drapes hung open in the bay window. The professor followed Williams to the far end of the room and watched as Williams placed his supper down on the light wooden table.

Donna closed the front door after dropping the two cases next to the wooden coat stand. She was about to enter the open door on the right when Williams came through.

'Go in, I'll put the kettle on.'

She noticed his demeanour had changed since the hotel, he seemed more upbeat.

'Are we doing the right thing?' she asked in a low voice.

'Absolutely, the professor said, we now have a permanent base to work out of.'

'And what about if he goes into one of his moods again?' Donna asked.

Before the professor had chance to answer, a small square door in the wall, facing the table opened.

'I won't, and I've apologised for that, Williams said offering a teapot through the serving hatch.

Donna retrieved the teapot and placed it in the centre of the table, followed by a small milk jug and matching sugar pot. She felt a little embarrassed that Williams had heard her comments to the professor. Williams re-joined them at the table, after collecting cups and saucers from the cabinet that stood up the wall next to the table. Donna poured them all a drink and watched as Williams tucked into his fish and chips straight from its wrappings of yesterdays newspapers.

'I have been working on a little theory,' the professor said, watching William's tuck into his meal.

'I'm listening,' Williams said, juggling a hot chip in his mouth.

'Well, most crimes are perpetrated by people that know the area and feel comfortable in.'

'True,' Williams said.

'But we are not dealing with the norm, are we,' Donna said picking up the cup.

'Yes, but he will still want to operate in an environment that he is ok with,' the professor said.

'He's right,' Williams said pointing a finger at the professor, juggling another hot chip.

'So, you think he's close?' Donna asked.

'I do, I think if we say maximum of about ten miles from the centre of the two crimes, I believe he will be somewhere in there.'

'That's a huge area, even for a full investigation and all its resources available.'

'So what chance do the three of us have, well two and a half really,' donna said looking at Williams.

'True, I do need to be at work most of the time.'

Williams leaned back in the chair. The effects of the whisky had pretty much worn off and he felt better for having a full stomach. He rapped the few chips he had left and dumped the wrappings in the bin. He returned to the table to see Donna and the professor searching for their current location on a map that nearly covered the table.

Williams looked at the map for a few seconds before placing his finger to the left of the centre.

'This is us,' he told them.

He looked over it some more before dropping his finger down again.

'This is the first murder and here is the one from last night,' he said pointing to a third location.

'Good, good,' the professor said circling the three of them.

He looked at the bottom of the map for the scale. He placed his finger next to it moving his head slightly side to side, as if he was working out the measurements he wanted. He moved back to the centre of the two circles and moved out to the left before placing the tip of the pencil down and drawing a circle, ruffly the size of a tea plate.

The three of them looked at it in silence.

'That's a large area,' Williams said, taking a drag from his cigarette.

'True, the professor said, but we can narrow it down quite a bit by removing all the places we know are occupied.'

'And how are we going to do that?' Donna asked.

'The three of us, it would take more than a month to visit all the properties in that circle,' Williams said staring at the map.

'We don't need to visit all of them, just the ones that are isolated,' the professor said, while rolling the pencil between his fingers.

'Could we get a list of the working farms?' donna asked holding the cup with one hand and her other hand underneath it.

The two of them looked at Williams through the smoke that was surrounding him.

'I'm not on the case remember,' he said looking back at them.

The three of them returned to the map, just standing staring at it, all of them lost in their own thoughts.

Williams was the first to speak. He had had enough for one day. He doubted the cigarette and showed them their rooms and where the bathroom was and called it a night. He bayed them goodnight and turned in, wondering if he had done the right thing by asking them back.

CHAPTER 34

06:30 and Williams was woken by the beeping sound that plagued his mornings. He leaned over and pressed the snooze button, the button that everyone hated, but also loved in equal measure. The button that ended their night's sleep but would also give a few more minutes comfort and rest before what was planned needed to be done.

Williams went through his morning routine and headed downstairs.

'In here detective,' came the familiar voice of the professor.

'You been up all night?' he asked as he entered the living room to see the professor sitting at the table in a fine green housecoat.

'No, I get up at six every morning, and I don't need an alarm clock.'

The table had cups and saucers placed out with the teapot placed in the middle. A crock toast holder sat next to it with four halves of toast that had been cut into triangles sitting in.

'I hope you don't mind, but I thought it would be nice, you know, for inviting us to stay.'

'I don't really have time,' Williams told him.

'Then you should make time, I always start my day with tea and toast, gives you time to think on the day ahead,' the professor said as he poured Williams a cup.

Williams joined him at the table, he could see he had gone to a lot of trouble, and it would be nice for a change, rather than the usual rushing out the door.

'There you go,' the professor said as he passed Williams the cup of fresh tea.

Williams spooned in a single sugar and a dribble of milk.

'How you getting to work?'

'Taxi will take me to the hotel, what are you two up to today?'

'This and that.'

Williams didn't like the sound of that, but there was nothing he could do about it. He still had a job to do and bosses to answer too. The horn outside told him it was time to go.

'Just stay out of trouble,' Williams said before placing the cup down and heading out.

A slight north wind was blowing, leaving a slight chill in the air. Williams sat in the front, pulling the visor down to obscure the low sun shining directly at him. It was a lovely clear morning and the drive to the hotel gave him time to think, had he done the right thing last night. He paid the driver and climbed into his own car. His mind was on the day ahead, what with the new people in town and no doubt taking over the station.

He slowed as he passed the newsagents and looked at the front of the papers that were outside, all stacked up neatly on metal racks. He noticed that none of them had ran with the murders that they had said they were going to publish, some high up strings had been pulled to make that happen he thought.

Outside the station was quiet, no reporters meant only one thing, the story had been buried, he wondered what was offered in return, what scoop would they have prior knowledge too. Has long as it didn't involve him, he didn't care. The station was quiet, and people were keeping their heads down, no doubt word had spread about there new visitors. He made his way upstairs and stopped at the incident room, he couldn't believe his eyes, all the detectives were at their desk quietly working, he was a little puzzled. He turned and entered his office; Jackson was in too. Williams was the last one, had he missed something.

'What's going on?' he asked.

'We all got phone calls last night and were told to be in by seven this morning.'

'By who's orders?' Williams asked, placing his coat on the wooden stand.

Jackson poked his finger up towards the ceiling.

Williams knew exactly what he meant.

'Have you been assigned to our new friends then?' Williams asked.

'No one's said anything about that sir.'

Williams understood, it was a show for the new guests, how the super ran a tight ship.

'So, what have we got then?' Williams asked, as he sat at his desk.

'Not a lot, we are going to charge them two for burgling the off-licence, if you want to join us sir?'

'Not really,' Williams said, his mind on other things.

'It's a done deal, they were caught on the premises,' Williams said as he watched Jackson leave the room.

For some reason the normal day to day didn't seem to have the appeal anymore, the murders had taken over his daily thoughts. He decided to poke his nose in, after all he was the lead detective, and it was his station.

He walked past the detectives, some on phones, some with paperwork. The door at the rear was closed, he was going to knock but decided against it, it would give the impression they were in charge; he knew the super had their backs, but he didn't want to give them the luxury of everyone dancing to their tune.

He pushed the handle down and pushed the door open. Two were sitting at a long desk to the right. They both turned and looked at him as he entered.

'How can I help?' Andrews asked, looking annoyed that he had entered.

'Just seeing if there is anything we can do,' Williams said, knowing they didn't want any interference.

'No! we are good thanks, came the reply, if we need anything we will let you know.'

'My door is always open,' Williams said, being a little facetious.

'Can you knock next time,' Andrews said, noticing William's tone.

'No, Williams said blatantly, there's only one door I knock,' he said before backing out and closing the door.

He returned to his office, not with any purpose, it wasn't like he had anything to do, or nothing pressing anyway. An hour had passed when one of them entered his office and informed him he was requested by Andrews. Williams followed him to the office at the corner of the incident room.

'I need these places checked out,' Andrews said, holding out two sheets of paper.

'What for?' Williams asked, looking at the names and addresses on them.

'I need to know if they have seen anything suspicious or out of the ordinary.'

'Like what?'

'Anything, like late comings and goings, anything out of the ordinary.'

'I'll put some men on it then.'

'There will be more men arriving in the next couple of days, so I'm going to need a bigger room,' Andrews told him.

'There's a conference room upstairs, but it's filled with filing cabinets and desks.'

'It will need to be made ready,' Andrews told him.

Williams didn't answer, he turned and closed the door. He looked at the papers and handed them to Jackson.

'Split these into five,' he told him.

Jackson did as he was ordered and copied the names and addresses down on five different pieces of paper. All sheets had equal names and addresses on, and he offered them back to Williams.

'Hand them out,' Williams said, nodding to the incident room opposite.

'Sir,' Jackson said turning away.

'And tell them they are to report directly to me.'

Williams folded and pocketed the original. He made a quick call and re-placed the receiver as Jackson returned.

'I'm going out, Williams told him.'

'Where you going, if someone asks?'

'Making enquiries.'

Williams left the station. He had his own investigation that needed his time, he wasn't going to waste it sitting at his desk taking orders from strangers.

CHAPTER 35

Mid-day and the stranger sat watching the struggle of life play out through the grime ridden windows that overlooked the rear of the old farmhouse. He watched as the cat had played the waiting game before moving into a better position for the finale. The two rats had been coming and going without any idea they were being watched or stalked would be a more accurate way of describing it.

Slowly the predator moved into place, waiting for the right time to make its move, slowly and carefully at first before the lightning attack that the stranger knew was coming.

He too knew the game, something he had polished over the centuries. The beginning was easy, but has he had observed the humans get more and more sophisticated, he had needed to change his approach, not something the cat had needed to worry about, but in the end the two were no different really.

Both predators needed to quench the thirst that built to an uncontrollable struggle that needed fulfilling at all costs. The stranger looked on as one rat exited followed by the second, blissfully unaware that one of them wouldn't make it home again.

The cat moved slowly, keeping low to the ground, its position next to the rubbish that had built up prior to the stranger taking possession of the abandoned house. The stranger had no where better to be than where he was right now. He watched as the clouds moved across the sky casting shadows, breaking the brightness of the mid-day sun.

The cat was primed for the final act, one that would end with one of life's struggles being enacted right in front of him. The two had waited for thirty minutes or so before the two rats appeared from under the broken-down fence, slowly they made their way across the dirty concrete yard that weeds had taken hold of with any crack that became available.

The stranger watched as the cat readied itself. Then it happened, the first rat took evasive action darting to its right just in time, missing the nose of the cat by millimetres. The second wasn't so lucky. A split-seconds delay had cost it its life. Was it that the first rat had obscured its view, or had it hesitated, or was it always going to end that way, who really knows, but one thing was for sure, the stranger had only admiration for the predatory instincts of the cat.

He watched as the cat walked off slowly with the dead body of its prize hanging from its mouth. The prize for all the patience and ferocity that the stranger knew he was capable of too.

The excitement was filling him, later that night he too would be playing the game. Not quite like the cat, a little more tactful, but with the same outcome all the same. He knew the lay of the land, he had done his due diligence. For now, he had to wait. The early days were hard, but with experience comes knowledge and he knew the right time to strike, just like the cat had honed its skills over many a hunt.

CHAPTER 36

Williams turned the key and stepped inside. He could hear talking coming from the Livingroom as he stepped in looking at Donna and the professor sitting at the table.

'What you doing?' Williams asked stopping next to them.

'After your phone call this morning.'

'While we were waiting,' donna said, interrupting the professor.

Williams looked at her but decided to ignore the comment and looked back at the professor.

The professor too ignored the comment and continued.

'We have been going over some of the books we got from the library, its amazing,' the professor said before Williams cut in.

'I need you to find these places on the map.'

The professor was immediately drawn to the pieces of paper Williams withdrew from his pocket.

'What is it?' the professor asked.

'These are the places the MOD have earmarked for possible places they think he might be staying.'

Donna looked at Williams but didn't say anything.

The professor closed the book and removed it from the table, replacing it with the map.

'I'll leave it with you, I need to get back.'

'Yes yes,' the professor said, not taking his eyes from the map, running his finger from place to place, searching for the first address.

Williams left them to it, he needed to return before awkward questions were asked.

He stopped next to the side entrance and passed the desk sergeant, who nodded as he passed. He climbed the stairs and passed the incident room; it was all quiet and Jackson was sitting at his desk not doing anything.

'Sir, that information you said you wanted before it's handed over,' Jackson said, holding out a light brown folder.

Williams took it and placed it on his desk before hanging his coat.

'Go and get us a cuppa,' Williams said, picking up the file.

Williams opened it and started reading, most of it was what he expected. There was a couple of things of interest, but one stood out. He waited for Jackson to return.

'Who was on this one?' he asked.

Jackson looked at the address and returned to his desk. He rummaged through some papers before turning back.

'It was brown sir; do you want me to fetch him?'

'No,' Williams said getting up from his seat and heading for the incident room.

Detective Paul brown was sitting at the far end by the window. He was of slim build and a clean-cut sort of guy.

'Paul, you spoke to someone earlier, you put, seen tyre tracks leading to the farmhouse,' Williams handed over the paper.

'Yes sir, the local farmer said a couple of days back there were fresh tyre tracks, but he didn't think much of it as he knew the developers were scouting the area for more land to buy up.'

'Did he say anything else.'

'No sir, accept the place has been abandoned for as long has he can remember.'

Williams returned to his desk and scribbled down the address and pocketed it. He passed the detectives and opened the door. The three were still sitting there as he stepped in and stopped next to Andrews.

'The information you wanted.'

'Thank you,' Andrews said taking it from him.

'Like I said, we should be working on this together.'

'Not my call, how's the room coming along?' he asked.

'Cleared out by tomorrow.'

'Thank you,' Andrews said, before turning away and opening the file.

Williams turned and left, closing the door loudly, not a slam but loud enough to show his annoyance at being used has no more than a gofer.

CHAPTER 37

Williams parked on the road in front of his house, the drive still occupied with the hired car. He stepped into the smell of a roast coming from the kitchen.

'Detective chief inspector, hope you don't mind, we decided to cook.'

'No,' Williams said following the professor into the Livingroom.

Donna was setting the table; Williams noticed the map and addresses had been folded neatly and placed on the dresser.

'His idea,' donna said, placing the last of the cutlery down.

'Makes a change from the local chippy,' Williams said taking in the smell that he hadn't smelled since his mother had passed away many years ago.

'Go and sit, it won't be long,' the professor told him before leaving them and heading back to the kitchen.

'I didn't know he could cook,' Williams told Donna, as the two headed to the sofa.

'Actually, he's a very good cook.'

'If it tastes as good as it smells, were in for a treat.'

Williams sat next to the fire in the single chair with Donna on the sofa.

'Did you find the addresses I gave you?'

'Yes, they are all circled.'

'Good, I have more information.'

The professor passed them, heading to the cabinet that held an old radio that looked like it was from the days before TV. The professor turned the dial until he found the station he was looking for. Classical music filled the air and the professor looked happy with himself before returning to the kitchen.

'I don't think I have seen him happier than in the last couple of days.'

'He's certainly making himself at home,' Williams said, are all professors like him?'

'No, most I have met are very serious all the time,' she said raising an eyebrow.

The two could hear the banging of saucepans and the tap running.

'I should see if he needs a hand,' donna said before leaving him alone.

A few minutes later the professor returned.

'Can you collect them, Donna will pass them through the hatch,' the professor said as he headed for the table.

Williams followed and did as was asked. The three sat with a roast chicken and veg, with homemade Yorkshire pudding. Donna was right, Williams thought, as he savoured every mouthful. It wasn't until they had finished, and the table was cleared before the conversation returned to why they were there.

The professor was first. He collected the map and opened it. Williams could see the circles that had been made. He removed the piece of paper from his rear pocket.

'According to one of my detectives, this place might be of interest to us.'

'How so?' Donna asked.

'A local farmer seen fresh tyre tracks recently, but the place has been abandoned long ago.'

The professor took the paper and found the address on the map. It was at the far edge of the circle that he had made the night before.

'Well, its inside the parameters,' The professor said looking through his glasses that were perched on the end of his nose.

'So far it's the only lead we have.'

True the professor said, not taking his gaze from the map.

'So, what do we do?' Donna asked, with a look of trepidation on her face.

'Well, we must go and take a look of cause,' the professor said glancing at them over the top of his glasses.

'Hold on, this is an active investigation by the MOD, if we get caught, we are in big trouble,' Williams said, staring at the professor.

'I agree,' Donna chimed in with.

Williams wasn't so sure she was backing him because of the MOD, he figured she was more worried in case they were correct, and it really was the right place.

The phone in the lounge started ringing. Williams left the two of them and answered it.

'I've got to go out,' he said on returning.

'What for?' Donna asked.

I left a message that if anyone calls complaining of anything out of the ordinary, they are to contact me at once.'

'And?' Donna asked.

'Possible burglary or someone is casing the place.'

'Like the old lady you mean.'

'No, this was a few weeks ago, the old timer rang to see why he hasn't had any follow up.'

'We will come with you.'

'This is work, not this,' Williams said pointing to the table.

'Better to be safe than sorry,' the professor said retrieving his stick from the seat he had laid it across.

How could he say no, they had just cooked him a lovely meal and the two were out of their seats before he had chance to object. They will just have to stay in the car he thought to himself, but no need to tell them that until the get there, no need to listen to the professor explaining how it would be better if the more people he had the more help and all that, like two heads are better than one and so on. Williams couldn't believe he had the two of them in toe as he set off. A few days ago, he wouldn't even have dreamed of what he was doing.

CHAPTER 38

The barn doors were pulled open easily as the stranger stepped in and reversed the car out. Stopping and closing them wasn't something he was too bothered about; all he could think of was what would be coming in the short time ahead.

The car bumped along slowly, the full moon glistening brightly in the sky, just how he felt with the anticipation of what was to come. He slowed as he approached the place he would conceal the car. The walk to his destination was filled with excitement, just how the cat must have felt before the finale.

The house was situated just off the main road, secluded from any passing motorists; just has he had planned. Like all his choices these days, seclusion was his first priority. He knew this would probably be his last feast for a while, he maybe should have moved on after the previous one, but he had already scouted the place and one more wouldn't make that much of a difference.

He stopped and turned, just to be sure. Just as he thought, nothing. He walked up the path, past the tall hedge that was easily as tall as him and gave great concealment. The place was dark, the solid wooden door and windows that were showing no light due to the heavy curtains that hung in the bay windows.

The silence was broken with two loud knocks from the heavy knocker that hung in the middle about head hight. The stranger waited, listening for the tell tail sign that someone was home. It wasn't long before he heard the distinctive sound of someone moving slowly, getting closer and closer. He had to calm himself, the excitement rising.

The door opened slowly, the light penetrating the darkness and a figure of an elderly man standing there.

'Yes,' he said, looking a little happy that someone had came to see him, maybe the first visitor he had had in ages.

The stranger used his old technique, humans were always ready and willing to help someone in need, what strange creatures they are he thought to himself, but that was to his advantage, he used their good nature against themselves. The old man turned and headed back down the hallway, the stranger followed, closing the world out. He listened carefully to pick up any noises that would alert him if anyone other than the old man was in the house. The stranger followed him through the door on the left; a warm glow was coming from the open fire. A game show of some sorts was showing on the black and white TV that was perched on a small table in front of an old Fred bare seat with wooden arms.

'The phone is over there,' the old man said pointing to a dining table that was filled with newspapers.

More papers had been stacked underneath and more were pushed into the corner of the room. The stranger turned slowly, watching as the old man made himself comfortable. He opened his coat and raised his head slightly, the old man looked at him with a puzzled look on his face. Slowly fear swept over the old man's face as what he was witnessing didn't make sense, how could it, all his years and beliefs told him it was impossible, but here it was, happening in front of him.

The stranger could see the fear on the old mans face, but he had no remorse for what he was about to do, why would he, he was a predator standing over his prey.

Blood dripped down the pearly white fangs as the stranger stood upright, the elation he felt couldn't be beaten, nothing came close to the feeling he had right at that moment. He felt his legs give a little as the effects started to take hold, he knew it would only be temporary, but it was worth it. He grabbed the mantelpiece, taking some of the weight from his legs. That's when he heard the distinctive sound from outside. He knew this was the only time he was vulnerable; he had done his reconnaissance and knew the old man lived alone.

Car doors closed, almost in unison, but he picked up the distinct sound of three doors being closed, followed a few seconds later by the front door being knocked. He was trapped and he knew it and he was in no fit state to do anything about it.

CHAPTER 39

'It's the next left,' the professor said, holding his finger on the map.

Williams turned left as instructed and slowed as he approached the isolated house.

'Doesn't look like anyone's home,' Donna said from the rear seat.

'I'll go and knock,' Williams said, killing the engine.

'Good idea let's do that,' the professor said.

'Hold on,' Williams said, but it was too late, the pair of them had flung the doors open and were already halfway out before he could protest.

There were words to be had after this he thought to himself, and he would make sure they understood the message loud and clear, but for now he had no choice. Williams followed them up the path and passed them as he stopped at the door.

'Let's get one thing straight, I will be the one doing the talking,' he said before knocking.

'Of cause, you won't even know we are here,' the professor said, leaning on his stick.

Williams doubted that, but they were there like it or not.

The three waited silently when Williams and Donna thought they heard a noise coming from inside. The two looked at each other.

'What?' the professor asked.

'I think someone's coming,' Donna told him.

They waited before Williams knocked again, making sure there could be no mistakes.

They waited some more before Williams stepped back and surveyed the front of the house. He decided to try the gate to the left, giving him access to the rear. The latch lifted allowing the gate to open a little, something was wedged behind it. Williams pushed on it. Whatever was behind moved, he pushed again, listening to the scraping sound coming from behind the gate. He stopped pushing when he had enough space to squeeze through. He slid in between the gate and the wall, that's when he seen the metal dustbin that had been used to secure the gate. He walked to the rear, maybe the occupant was tone deaf and didn't hear the door, he didn't want to walk away without making sure he had tried.

To Williams surprise the rear door was open and the kitchen was in darkness.

'Hello,' he shouted, not entering, he didn't have probable cause.

Williams jumped as he felt a hand on his shoulder.

'I told you to wait,' he said, looking at Donna standing next to him, and the familiar sound of the professor bringing up the rear, the click, click clicking getting closer.

'Do not follow me in, just stay here,' words were going to be said for sure.

Williams stepped in. The kitchen was in darkness, he picked up that to his left a cooker stood between some cabinets and the sink was under the window. He made his way to the door directly in front of himself and turned the handle.

'Hello,' he shouted again, looking down the hallway facing the door he had just been standing at.

Light from an open door was on his right, illuminating the hallway. He stepped to it and peered in. He turned and immediately returned to the back door.

'Did you see or hear anything?' he asked, his head darting about, looking left to right.

'No, why?' Donna asked.

The professor could see the expression on his face, 'is there a problem?' he asked.

'You could say that.'

Williams walked down the garden, even in the darkness he could see the broken-down fencing, and the trees next to the property that would allow easy access or escape.

Williams tried the door to a brick out-house, it was locked.

'What's the problem?' the professor asked again.

'Follow me,' he said passing them and heading through the kitchen. The two followed in single file, not really knowing what was going on.

'Ow dear,' the professor said standing next to Williams, looking down at the dried-up corpse.

Donna appeared to the side of Williams. She grabbed his arm on seeing what once would have been a person.

'The noise,' she said gripping his arm tighter.

Williams nodded.

'What noise?' the professor asked.

'We need to get out of here,' Williams told them.

'Shouldn't we call it in?' the professor asked.

'No we shouldn't, were not supposed to be here, remember.'

Williams turned and headed for the back door, knowing if they got caught, he was in big trouble.

CHAPTER 40

The car stopping and doors closing spooked the stranger. The knocking at the front door gave him a decision to make, stay and hope they went away or get out. He stumbled from the fireplace, past the dried-up corpse to the table, his legs weak and not feeling his own. The stack of papers were knocked over as he grabbed the table, trying not to hit the floor. He made it to the hallway when the door knocked again, this time much louder. He seen the back door, doing his best to stay upright, he stumbled over, luckily the key was in the lock, or he would have been trapped. The back door was opened has he heard the side gate being forced. He needed concealment, standing and fighting wasn't an option, not while he was in this state, he knew he had another five minutes or so before he would regain his full strength.

He made it to the side of the outhouse, leaning on it hard. He knew the full moon would give them good vision and waiting wasn't an option. He pushed along the side of the fencing until he came to a broken bit and passed through, stumbling into the trees on the opposite side and dropping behind a thick trunk. The silence was broken when he heard one of them come running from the house, he couldn't quite hear what was being said, but he watched as one of them darted down the garden, looking in all directions. Luckily, he had returned to the house, and he was relieved he hadn't been seen.

Slowly he felt the strength returning, he wasn't quite there yet, but he felt better that if he needed to, he could at least stand and hold his own. He listened as he heard the three of them leaving, something he needed to do, no doubt they would call the police and the place would be crawling within the next thirty minutes.

The car was parked on the far side of the trees. A little more strength had returned, and he could stand upright and take in the surroundings. What was puzzling was that they hadn't stayed, maybe the body spooked them, but why drive away, why not sit and wait for the police to show up. In the end it didn't really matter, the fact he was away and his strength returning was all that really mattered to him, in a few days he would be gone, and this place would only be a distant memory, like all the others.

He made his way from the trees and started the car. The drive home gave him time to think about his next move. Abandoned properties were getting harder to come by these days, too much development he thought. He had played with the idea of fitting in with the locals, but that would mean he would have to interact with them, and the truth was, he just didn't like them, too nosy, why couldn't they just keep themselves to themselves.

He reversed the car into the barn and closed the doors. His strength had returned, and he felt elated once again, the close call was one of the hazards he had to endure now and again.

He sat looking out of the grimy windows to the back yard, the life and death struggle that took place that afternoon was gone, but he knew it would all play out again very soon. He wasn't sentimental, but he had enjoyed watching the drama unfold, maybe the next place wouldn't be so entertaining.

CHAPTER 41

Present day

'Mr Williams, you were so close to actually catching him in the prosses,' the taller one of the two said.

'Well yes, but what we didn't know was, what sort of trouble we could have been in, it wasn't until later that we fully understood his capabilities, and let me tell you now, we were lucky, very lucky.'

'But surely you had some inkling of what you were up against?'

'Not really, how could I, at the start I was in denial, as the case moved on, yes, I did believe… with what the evidence showed we were dealing with, something not of, Williams paused for a moment, trying to think of the right words, certainly nothing of what I could have envisaged,' he finally said.

'But Miss Wade and the professor were.'

'Ow yes, they were fully convinced right from the start of what we were dealing with, but all their knowledge was from books.'

'And yet you continued with the investigation.'

'Of course, the evidence, I followed the evidence.'

'And the more you looked at the evidence.'

'yes, the more we looked the more we, well the more I became convinced that we were correct.'

'When did you realize how lucky you had been?'

'It was after the two deaths, sometimes I wish I would have never gone to oxford and just passed it over to you lot and walked away.'

Williams looked lost for a few moments, lost in his own thoughts.

'If you would like to take a break?' the shorter one said.

'No, its fine,' Williams said and continued with his recollection.

CHAPTER 42

Williams stopped at the front entrance to the station, it was early, and he had passed on the professor's breakfast, last night still playing on his mind. He hadn't called in the incident, too many questions, he had decided to send a couple of bobbies up that morning, he figured it would be safe enough, after all there was nothing left for him to return too, he had had what he came for. If it played out like he figured, he could make an appearance and then pass it over to the MOD.

The station was quiet, more the way it was before they arrived. He sat at his desk, nothing of urgency awaiting him. The words he was going to have, didn't materialise, didn't seem as important after what they had witnessed, another day maybe. For now, he only had one thing on his mind, getting back up to the house and dealing with the mess. He couldn't believe he had walked away from a crime scene without calling it in.

The three from the MOD were the first to arrive. They didn't stop for niceties, why would they, it wasn't like they were colleagues. The three disappeared into the back room without even looking in his direction. It was a good half an hour before the first of the detectives started to arrive, followed soon after by Jackson.

'Before you sit down, I want you to send a couple of officers up to this address.'

Williams handed over a note with the address of the property they were at last night.

'What for sir?' Jackson asked looking at the note.

'He thinks someone has been snooping around, just send a couple of bobbies up to reassure him.'

'Ok,' Jackson said, leaving him sitting on his own once again.

The first part done he thought. All he had to do now was wait for the call to come in, pop up and then pass it on.

Williams watched as Andrews exited the side room and headed his way.

'How you getting on with that room?' he asked.

No morning or how are you, straight to business, probably not used to having to ask for things. Williams had done his national service, so he knew how the army worked.

'On it this morning,' he said with a smile.

No point in banging heads, it was his station, even if they thought they had taken charge, things would get done when he said they would. Williams watched as he returned to his side room just as Jackson returned from downstairs.

Someone's going up this morning,' Jackson told him has he hung his coat.

It was a good hour before news came in that a detective was required. Williams played the innocent, what's all the fuss about, just send the doctor and all that. He ordered Jackson to bring the car around the front.

'What's all the fuss about?' the captain asked, after overhearing the conversation.

'A body has been found that's all, possible foul play.'

'Nothing to do with us, is it?' the captain asked.'

'Don't see how,' Williams replied before leaving him standing on his own.

Williams was happy to get out of the station, too much interference for his liking.

Jackson stopped behind a squad car at the front of the house and were met by a tall lanky officer.

'What we got?' Williams asked joining him on the pavement.

'Not quite sure sir,' he told him, looking a little puzzled.

Williams nodded his head and passed him. Jackson followed him through the front door and to the sitting room where the body was still in the same position as last night.

'Sir, what's going on?' Jackson asked.

'No idea, but we need to pass it over, get on to the station and pass on the message, they are needed.'

Jackson nodded and left the room.

'I may not be a detective, but this isn't normal,' the constable said looking at the dried-up corpse.

'You're right, but it's not our concern.'

'Still our patch though.'

'And we've been pulled, Williams said shrugging his shoulders, has the house been checked?'

'Yes sir, all clear.'

'Good, how did you get in?' Williams asked knowing full well.

'The back door was open.'

'I thought there were two of you?'

'Yes sir, jimmy found footprints in the soil where the fence is broken.

'You stay at the front door, no one in until the MOD get here.'

'Sir.'

Williams exited the back door just in time to catch the second constable coming back through the broken fencing.

'Well?' Williams asked.

'I had a look about for more footprints, but it's too overgrown.'

Williams bent down, easy a size twelve he figured, big feet usually meant big man.

'Ok, stay at the back door and wait for the MOD to arrive.

'Then what sir?'

'No idea, not my case.'

Williams walked down the side of the house and exited the gate. Last night's little escapade was covered, finding the body wouldn't help with the case one bit, he knew it wasn't going to be solved the usual way.

'Sir, they are on their way, and they want you to wait for them,' Jackson told him.

'Do they,' Williams said as he got in the car.

'Keys,' Williams said, holding out his hand as Jackson joined him.

'You're not waiting?'

'Not my case, I'll drop you back at the station.'

He wasn't going to wait around and take orders, he had done his two years national service and had his fill of taking orders, he had more pressing things on his mind.

Williams turned the car around when he seen the three newcomers that had been at the hotel, he couldn't forget them, how could he, it wasn't every day you seen men wearing make-up. The three looked like hikers, not like he cared, he had more pressing things on his mind.

CHAPTER 43

The stranger sat in his usual spot, surveying the back yard. The struggle of yesterday was about to play out again, but a different set of rules this time around. The resident black and white cat had locked eyes with a newcomer, the odds were more closely matched than yesterday's one-sided affair.

He watched as the staring contest took hold, neither wanting to break eye contact, neither wanting to make the first move, but inevitably one would. Thirty minutes had passed as both sized each other, maybe looking for a weakness, maybe not. He had seen it play out before, one would ultimately win the prize, the prize of a steady supply of food from the local rodents and birds. It had been a good hunting ground for the resident cat, just like the local area had been for him. But he knew his time was coming to an end, maybe it was for the resident cat too.

It was the resident cat that made the first move, dropping down from its favourite windowsill. The newcomer watched before trotting across the open yard, they both met in the middle, a ball of tangled legs and high-pitched noise breaking the silence. All about had gone quiet, as if the birds had perched for a ring side seat to the best show in town.

It was over in under a minute, fast, vicious, and no quarter given, but there could only be one winner, no second prize, winner takes all. He had seen enough struggles in his time, he had been in a few himself, luckily, he had always been on the winning side, so how the looser felt he couldn't know, and he had no intension of finding out.

Last night had been a close call, too close really, but if they had caught him at his most susceptible, would they have even known what to do with him, somehow, he didn't think so, and by the time they would have made a decision, his strength would have returned enough to deal with them, but nevertheless, it couldn't happen again, no more mistakes.

He sat watching as the victor sat up-right next to the pile of rubbish, ears in listening mode, a constant watching as the looser slowly limped off into the distance. It would be the last time he would see the struggle of life and death play out on the little piece of concrete, one that was nothing to anyone, but life and death for some.

The eery silence that followed the struggle had abated, the victor sat cleaning himself, stopping momentarily to survey the surroundings before continuing. A simple solitary life, much the same as his, he thought. One that he knew with the march of time was coming to an end. He had pondered about staying in England but with the march of progress, maybe it was time for a new start overseas, one that still held onto the old ways.

CHAPTER 44

Williams had dropped Jackson off as promised and returned home. Donna and the professor were sitting at the table.

'What's this?' he asked, looking down at what they were doing.

'After last night we thought we needed to take precautions,' donna said as she stood.

Williams sat in the vacated chair. 'How's this going to help?' he asked picking up a bottle of water.

'Not just any old water, holy water,' the professor said taking the bottle from him.

'And this?' Williams asked picking up a wooden stake from the centre of the table.

'I have done my research; the stake is the only way to end this.'

'So, the visit to the church was for the water and crucifix.'

'The water yes, the crucifix is mine,' the professor said, tapping his hand on the brass cross sitting next to him.

'And these three items are all we have to stop him?'

'It's all we need.'

'That's what I said,' Donna said placing a fresh cup of tea in front of him.

'Maybe we should continue with the search of finding him and then pass it on to the MOD,' she said sitting down next to Williams.

'No, they wouldn't have a clue, I bet they think they are going to arrest him or something, no, it has to be us that stops him,' the professor said placing the items in a black leather bag that looked just like the ones you would see doctors carrying in old movies.

'That address you gave us, I think we should take a look tonight,' the professor said, after placing the bag on the floor.

'And what if he's there, then what?' Donna asked.

'We end it,' the professor said.

Donna looked at Williams, was she the only one thinking straight, or had they both lost their mind.

'I think the professor's right, we go take a look this evening.'

'And what about all the stories you have told me?' She asked.

'That's why it needs to be us, they don't know what they are dealing with,' the professor said picking up the cup from the saucer.

She couldn't believe she was going along with it; the professor thinks he's on a treasure hunt, and Williams is on his own personal race with the MOD. Neither of them had thought it through, the consequences if they were right could be death, and most probably theirs.

'Tell him?' she said, looking at the professor.

'Tell him what?' The professor asked.

'How strong he is.'

'We don't know that for sure.'

'Know what?' Williams asked, glancing between the pair.

'I'll tell you, Donna said, he's as strong as five men.'

She left the information hanging in the air, hoping that maybe, Williams would reconsider about this evening's excursion. Williams looked at the professor.

'Some manuscripts I have read, do say they have, a few seconds passed before he continued, un-natural strength.'

'Well, I have delt with big guys before,' Williams replied.

Donna conceded, it didn't matter what he was told, they were going.

Williams sipped at the tea before asking the professor a question.

'How do you know all this stuff?'

'If you know what you are looking for, it's not that hard to find.'

'So what, you pop down the library and ask for any books on vampires?'

'Not really, a good sauce is folklore, there maybe only a passing line, or two, but when you find bits here and there, a picture starts to emerge. The test is trying to find out what has merit and what doesn't.'

'And how do you do that?'

'By cross referencing it of cause,' he said, looking at him like, what a silly question to ask.

'And of cause, there is the personal accounts.'

'What personal accounts?' Williams asked.

'Letters, correspondence between families, that sort of thing.'

'And how do you get hold of that sort of stuff?'

'Contacts, people that know people, that sort of thing.'

Williams looked at the professor in his tweed jacket and the glasses sitting on the end of his nose, a driven man Williams thought. His methodical way would have probably made him a good detective, or maybe anything he put his mind too.

Williams finished the last of his tea and headed back to the station with one thing on his mind, what Donna had said about his strength, she was probably wrong, maybe last night had spooked her. He stopped at the side entrance and passed the custody sergeant, who nodded as he passed. Jackson was at his desk when Williams entered.

'Sir we have a hit and run in town,' Jackson told him.

'Well, it's time you started to up your game, I'll be here if you need me.'

Jackson looked a little shocked, but he didn't wait for a second invite, it was his time to show what he could do, and he was going to take it.

'Remember, keep me informed,' Williams told him as he left the office at pace.

Williams had a few things to do, one of them was the room up-stairs that needed sorting before tomorrow, when the troops would be arriving.

CHAPTER 45

Williams stepped out of the station, and straight into the pouring rain, the clouds had been building all day, and finally they had broken. He had heard the MOD talking about the property he was going to visit that night, they wouldn't go until tomorrow he figured, so he would beat them to it, strike for him.

The rental car was still on the drive as he pulled up, the wipers struggling to move the water from the windscreen. He made a dash for the front door, key in hand. He shook his coat and hung it, water dropping to the floor. There was no smell of food in the air, not like the previous evening.

'Good evening,' the professor said on seeing him enter, looking his usual jolly self.

Williams noticed Donna looked a little apprehensive, but he didn't say anything, no point in making a thing of it.

'I thought we could get something to eat after,' the professor said.

He didn't mention it, no need, they all knew what he was on about. Williams looked at Donna sitting on the sofa, she couldn't hide how she felt.

'You don't have to come?' he said, offering her a way out.

'We started this together.'

Good, that's settled then,' the professor said, jumping on Donnas words as he got up from the single chair that was Williams's favourite.

He picked up the black bag and walking stick. Williams didn't know why he would bring it, maybe it made him feel safe, maybe reassurance for Donna, maybe a bit of both.

Williams ran around the front of the car after making sure the professor was in and out of the driving rain. He felt droplets of water running down his neck and his hair was wet from the extra few seconds it took to get in the car.

The car was started, and the heater put on full to clear the windows. Slowly they pulled off, heading into the unknown.

The professor was on map duty, something he had taken upon himself, no discussion or debate, his job, his input. Williams hadn't argued, truth is he wasn't to bothered, and the fact he was quite good at it made it easier for him.

They headed in the opposite direction from the city, street lighting disappearing as they made their way along the roads that were struggling to drain the water. Twenty minutes later and they sat in front of the old, abandoned farmhouse.

'There's no way anyone is staying there,' Williams told them, using his hand to clear the condensation from the windscreen.

'Are you going to drive up,' the professor said, looking at the road that was in the shape of an S, that stopped at the rear of the property.

'No, we walk from here.'

'Why?' Donna asked.

'The car would alert anyone of our arrival,' Williams said, looking at her in the rear-view mirror.

'Good point, the professor said, stealthy approach would work better.'

Williams had an inside chuckle to himself, how stealthy could they be with the clicking of his cane, and it certainly wouldn't be fast.

'I thought you would approve,' Williams said, allowing him his moment.

The rain had slowed some, but only from a deluge to a steady downpour, one that would allow the drainage to cope.

'Can I ask a question?' Donna said.

They both craned their necks.

'Sure,' Williams said looking at her.

'If you're sure there's no one staying there, why bother?'

'I don't think anyone would be staying there, but if we drive away, we will always be wondering until we find him,' Williams replied.

'Very true, the professor chimed in with,' nodding his head in approval.

The three stood next to the car, looking up at the farmhouse. It was the professor that started off first. A man that knew more than most, but still with the drive to complete what he had come to do.

CHAPTER 46

The stranger had sat all day in the same spot. The struggle of life had played out in front of him, with the resident cat now perched on its favourite windowsill. He had watched the clouds building in the distance, until they had finally broken. The rain closing in was how he felt about his time at the farmhouse, the inevitability that the time had come to move on, just as it was inevitable the rain would move in.

He left the chair and made his way to the barn, no luggage or belongings, no remorse for what had conspired with his time there, just another time in his very long life, one that he had not asked for, but one that had given him great privileges, but had also come with great cost. He had stopped feeling sorry for himself a long time ago and accepted what he was, a predator that feasted on humans.

The short walk up to the barn was along the muddy path that he had made with the car tyres. He stepped into the barn just has he heard the sound of a car slowing and leaving the lane, he tracked it until it came to a stop. Three exited and looked over the house. He watched as they pushed on the back door before one of them used his shoulder to force it open.

Did he ignore it and leave or wait. He decided to wait, if they seen him leave, they would no doute follow, that's if they where there for him, something he didn't see feasible. A few minutes later the three stepped out, eyeing the barn. He watched as they stood next to the tracks he had made, discussing them and pointing in his direction.

They made their way up, side by side. He stepped back from the door and jumped up the corner of the side wall and front, easily holding himself in the corner about fifteen feet above the ground.

He watched from his vantage point as the three entered, they all removed torches and started scanning the barn, their attention drawn to the car, how they only see things from their perspective, if only they had scanned the whole barn, including the roof space they would have taken away his advantage, but humans will be humans.

He dropped silently, falling to his soon to be prey below. The two nearest the front of the car was his intended target, how easy they were to hit. He landed directly on top of them. Without warning the two crumbled to the floor, like a house of cards with a hand being placed upon them. With one movement the second in line was hurtled through the air like a rag doll, landing up against the far wall and sliding down to the floor in a heap, not moving. The second of the two was pulled upright and with great ease his neck broken, the snapping sound echoing around the barn.

The sound of two-gun shots rang out, hitting the stranger in the chest. The impacts brought a smile to his face before leaping into the air and landing next to the third intruder.

One hand grabbed the wrist that held the gun, and a second hand was thrust around the throat, squeezing the larynges. A blow came down on the stranger's head from his opponent's free hand that held the torch. The stranger lifted his opponent into the air and slammed him to the floor, the impact knocking the gun from his grasp and expelling the air from his lungs.

The third of the intruders tried to scramble away, but it was futile, the stranger had total control of the situation. The stranger stepped over his prey, placing one knee in the centre of his back and grabbing him under the chin with both hands. With one pull the intruders back was broken, leaving him bent in a grotesque shape.

The stranger looked at the three new corpses lying around, should he have one last feast before he moved on to pastures new.

CHAPTER 47

Williams and Donna followed the professor up the hill, following the road until they were at the muddy path that led up to the barn that stood to the right of the house, set back away on its own.

'Why we stopped?' Donna asked, trying to pull her head down into her coat.

'Look,' the professor said pointing the light beam on the muddy tracks.

Williams followed the beam as the professor moved it left to right, then up at the barn.

'What we looking at?' Donna asked.

'The footprints,' Williams replied.

'I can't see any,' she said, leaning forward slightly.

That's because the rain has washed most of them away, but there are some partial prints left, see, Williams said pointing to the left track.

The professor pointed the beam to where a partial boot print had made an impression.

'We need to take a look,' Williams told them.

'I agree,' the professor said moving off to the left of the track.

Williams took the centre of the tyre tracks, mainly because he wasn't dressed in the correct footwear for these conditions, and the grass would give him better grip. The professor on the other hand was well equipped with his walking boots and cane. Donna followed behind Williams, trying her best to stop the rain from running down her neck.

Progress was slow as Williams slipped a couple of times, his smooth soled work shoes struggling. Donna didn't fair much better, a couple of times she had to grab hold of Williams's back to stop herself from falling flat on her face.

The three stopped at the entrance, the professor handing Donna the bottle of water he had removed from the bag. Williams didn't say anything, if it gave her some comfort then what the hell.

It was Williams that pulled the large wooden door open and stepping in first followed by donna, with the professor bringing up the rear. The three stopped as soon as they entered, what they were expecting wasn't what they found. Three light beams were pointing in different directions on the floor and to the left a dried-up corpse lay at the foot of the wall. The car they had come to find was sitting to the right with a body that had been bent into an un-natural shape lying by the rear tyre.

A leg was dropped over the side of the boot as the thing they were looking for stepped from the rear. The professor pointed the beam of light at him as he stood looking at them.

Donna felt the pit of her stomach rising, her heart rate doubling. Her mouth seemed to dry up instantly as she watched the man, thing, she didn't quite know which, straighten up in front of them.

'It's getting busy this evening,' he said looking at the three new arrivals.

A good ten seconds passed before the stranger spoke again, 'anyone got anything to say, seems a long way to come for silence.'

He was playing with them, he knew they caused him no threat and just like a cat would play with its prey, he was enjoying himself.

'Dreadful night,' he said, with a smile.

Williams wasn't sure what to think, it was speaking to them, gob smacked, struck dumb, petrified, all the emotions he could think of, he had all at once. He hadn't noticed Donna had grabbed his arm so tight that the imprints of her fingers would be around for a while.

'Why don't you close the door, frightful night out,' the stranger said, giving them a smile.

It had been a long time since he had had this much fun, and he was going to savour every moment of it. He bent down and with his left hand he picked up the deformed corpse and dropped it at the rear of the car. He picked up one of the torches that lay on the floor and pointed the beam at the dried-up body.

'He was tasty,' he said looking at them.

The fear on their faces was something to behold, 'well I take it that it was you that interrupted me the other night, 'he said panning the light beam between them.

'Well, you have found me, great work, now what, are you going to arrest me, take me in, read me my rights.'

Still they stood looking at him, his long black coat glistening now and again as the light reflected off it.

The stranger stepped forward, the light beam flicking from one terrified face to the next. It was the professor that made the first move, the brass cross removed from the bag before being dropped to the floor.

'I demand you to be gone in the name of the lord,' the professor said stepping forward to meet him.

The stranger pulled his hands across his face and turned slightly, not wanting to look at the cross.

The professor took another step closer, Williams and Donna watched in amazement, but it was short lived. The stranger took hold of the cross and removed it easily from the professor.

'Really,' he said, examining the cross before pushing the professor across the floor with one hand.

The cross was tossed to the floor beside the professor that had landed hard by the dried-up corpse. He took a step closer to Williams, with Donna half hiding behind him.

'And what have you brought to the party?' he said looking at Williams, who hadn't said, or more precisely didn't know what to say.

As the stranger stepped forward, it was Donna that reacted first. The bottle of water the professor had given her was thrust at his face. Instantly he stumbled backwards, both hands holding his face and a high-pitched squeal filling the barn. The two waited, was he going to remove his hands and start laughing at them, like the professor.

The stranger removed his hands, but he wasn't laughing like before, his face had started to bubble where the water had landed, like acid burning into him.

'You're going to pay for that!' he snarled at them.

Williams took a step forward to meet him as he closed the gap. The playfulness that he had started with was gone. He eyed Donna from behind Williams, intent on revenge for the audacity of her actions.

Williams went for the round house punch, but he was dispatched with ease and force in equal measure, the pain searing into his hip as he landed hard on the wall and came to rest beside the professor.

Donna held the bottle of water in front of herself, it was the only thing she had between herself and a surely gruesome death. The stranger circled to her left pinning her between the front of the car and side wall. With Williams and the professor on the opposite side of the barn and unable to help, she knew she was in big trouble.

CHAPTER 48

The three hikers had watched as the three had entered the barn and heard the high-pitched scream. They made their way up the tracks and pulled the barn door open. Two men were moving slowly at the left wall and a man dressed in a long black coat was standing next to a woman that had pinned herself to the wall on their right.

'Get out of here,' they heard one of the men to their left call out.

The hiker that opened the barn door headed over to Williams and the professor, bending down and helping Williams sit up against the wall.

'You need to go, you're in the wrong place mister,' Williams told him through gritted teeth.

'No, we are exactly where we need to be, he said before standing and turning to the stranger, who by this time had stepped away from Donna and was standing in the middle of the barn.

Williams watched as the female escorted Donna over to Williams, before joining her two companions that were now standing in front of the stranger. Donna helped the professor to his feet. Williams tried to join them but the pain in his hip was too much to bare.

'Lordan, we finally meet after all this time, Williams heard the one that helped him say.

'What's going on?' Donna asked.

The professor didn't answer, he stood watching the four of them, his concentration solely on them, so much so he never heard Donna's question.

'We see you have been busy of late,' the woman said.

'Some of us accept who we are,' the stranger said, giving her a dead stair.

'And these?' she said pointing over to the two corpses at the rear of the car.

'For later,' he said with a grin.

'And what about these three?' she asked.

'Help yourself, on me,' he said looking at Donna and the professor huddled by the wall, with Williams still sitting on the ground.

'That's not going to happen, the first of the three said, we have chosen a different path.'

'Then more fool you for not accepting what you are.'

'We accept what we are, but that doesn't mean we have to do it like you.'

'Maybe I enjoy it,' the stranger said.

'A little too much we think.'

'Does it matter, they are like sheep, fools they are.'

'Maybe so, but it's over.'

'Yes, I have decided to move on.'

'Can't let that happen.'

'You can't stop me, you know its forbidden,' he said with a smile on his face.

The third of them who had stayed quiet lept at him, but the stranger read it, side stepping and helping him on his way to the rear of the barn. The two reacted simultaneously, both taking hold of his mid-section and lifting him into the air and driving him to the ground. A large boot hit the first of the males in the chest, throwing him against the barn door, flinging it open.

The stranger stood, keeping hold of the woman, he was about to pick her up when the third male came in from behind like an animal leaping on all fours and charging the stranger from behind. The impact took him off his feet and the two landed on the floor, just as the woman lept into the air, her foot landing where the stranger's chest would have been, but he had read her move and rolled away.

Williams, Donna and the professor watched, terrified of what was taking place. Williams was helped to his feet, the pain excruciating, but he was up. The professors light beam illuminated the dust that had fallen from the roofbeams as the barn seemed to shake from the impact of the stranger being hurled at the wall opposite them. The high-pitched squeals only added to the fear they felt.

The three moved to the corner, waiting for there chance to make a run for it, or as best they could, to get to the car. The two males and the stranger were going toe for toe when the female picked up the black bag the professor had brought and stopped in front of them.

'We will pin him down and one of you will need to finish it,' she said removing the wooden stake and mallet.

She looked at the three of them and held out the tools for Donna to take.

Donna shook her head, too scared to talk.

'They are in no fit state,' she said thrusting them into her hands.

Williams and the professor looked at Donna who was shaking and looking back at them. Neither of them spoke, they watched as the stranger was hurled headfirst into the side of the car, the impact lifting the car of the floor and sending it sideways. The three were starting to take charge of the situation, Williams knew it was only a matter of time before they would have control of him, that's when he knew it would be Donnas turn, he looked at her standing next to the professor, somehow, he didn't think she could do it.

The two males picked up the stranger from the side

of the car, they lept into the air with the stranger between them and drove him into the floor, dust kicking up. That's when the call was made. The stranger lay between the two males who were holding him down by both arms.

Donna didn't move. She stood helplessly with the mallet and stake clutched to her chest. The female came over and grabbed her by the arm, pulling her over to the pinned down stranger that lay prostate on the floor.

'You need to end it,' donna was told.

The female took hold of Donna by the shoulders and looked into her eyes.

'Look at me, you can do this, don't think, just do,' she said keeping eye contact.

Did she have some sort of mind control, who knows, but it seemed to do the trick. Donna seemed to snap out of her trance and followed her to the stranger who was starting to come around slightly. The female sat on his legs while the two males held him tight. Donna bent down beside him and placed the tip of the stake on the centre of his chest.

'Don't think, just do,' donna was told again.

Donna lifted the mallet into the air just as the stranger's eyes opened. He looked directly at her.

'Do it,' she was told.

The first blow wasn't hard enough to completely go through. The stranger started thrashing left to right, the female struggling to hold his legs down.

'Again,' donna was instructed.

The blow was harder, one that sent the stake through the stranger's chest and drove it into the ground below. The three stood and stepped away taking Donna with them.

All six watched as the stranger lay, holding the wooden stake with both hands, the high-pitched squeal filling the barn.

Slowly the centre of the stranger's chest started to fall in on itself, like ash falling from the end of a cigarette. Both hands pulled and pushed at the stake that was holding him to the ground, like some sort of forcefield that was keeping the stake up-right, no matter how much he pulled and pushed, it didn't budge. The hole that formed around the stake grew, working outwards until his torso had completely disappeared followed by the rest of him.

A pile of ash had replaced him, leaving an outline of where he lay. Williams now drew his attention to the three newcomers with Donna standing next to them. What now he wondered, would they need to be silenced, no witnesses, no one to tell the tale of what had conspired over the last few days.

The three walked over, with donna following.

'Do you need help to your car?' the one that Williams figured was the leader, has he seemed to be doing most of the talking.

'No,' Williams said, his body shaking a little.

'Then we need to go,' he said.

'I have some questions,' the professor said stepping forward.

'Not today professor,' was the reply.

'You know me?'

'We like to keep an eye on people of interest.'

'But I have.'

The professor was cut off, 'a conversation for another time,' he was told.

'Miss Wade, what you did was very courageous, thank you, without you he would still be running around.'

'But why didn't you do it,' the professor asked looking at them.

'It's forbidden, if we were to have done it, then the fate that befell him, would have happened to the one of us that drove the stake in.'

The three left them standing and headed out into the rain. By the time the professor, Donna and Williams left the barn they were nowhere to be seen. Williams had commandeered the walking stick and the three made their way slowly down the tracks, glad to be leaving this place, but with more questions than when they arrived. But that was for another day. For now, they were just glad to be alive.

CHAPTER 49

Present day

The two men sat listening intently to every word Williams had said, like children engrossed in a good story, but it wasn't. Had they expected Williams to be so open and frank, probably not. Williams had given up being diplomatic years ago, probably after the death of his wife. Right now, he couldn't care less if they believed him or not, at his age what could they do.

'Where did the three, there was a little pause, Williams figured he wasn't quite sure what to address them as, hikers come from?' he finally said.'

'They had been watching us, they came to the house the following day.'

'You're joking,' the shorter one said.

'It was a bit of a shock when they walked through the door.'

'You let them in?'

'No, I didn't, I was recuperating on the sofa, the professor answered the door.'

'Well, that explains it,' the taller one said.

'Ow yes, he had many questions for them,' Williams said, moving slightly in the chair, maybe talking about it had triggered a memory.

'What did they want?' the taller one asked sitting forward.

'Well, first of all, they wanted to make sure we were all ok, it seems they had been tracking him for a while, but he had always given them the slip.'

'How did you feel to have them in the house?'

It was quite strange really, but I never felt scared of them, not like when we came face to face with him in the barn, you could sense the evil in him, the look made the hair on the back of your neck stand up, Williams paused a moment, you knew something bad was going to happen,' he finally said.

'They only came to see if you were, ok?'

'Yes, but the professor had a lot of questions.'

'Like what?'

'How it all started.'

'And did they say?'

'Yes, they confirmed what the professor had told me, the deal with the devil, the battle, but there was one other thing that they told us. A few days after the battle, after they had all returned home, everyone that had been cursed had turned on their own families and loved ones. The villages were littered with corpses. Most of them scattered after, but the ones that remained, were hunted and killed.'

'Did they say how many were left?'

'No.'

'Did they tell you anything else?'

They explained how it was them that had informed the professor, they had stumbled upon the farm, they had followed us to the other two incidents too. I'm glad they were following us, because I wouldn't be here today if it wasn't for them.'

Williams had noticed how the taller one had been glancing at the photo, that sat pride of place on the fire surround.

'That's the three of us,' Williams told him.

'You're wedding day?' he asked.

'Yes, I took some leave and went back to oxford with them, that's where me and Donna got close. A year later we were married, the professor was the best man.'

'I guess it had a happy ending.'

'Yes, we had a great life together, one that I wouldn't change.'

'And what happened to the hikers?'

'They left and we never seen them again. The professor seen the last of his days with me and Donna, he retired and moved up here with us, he was close to the children, maybe it was because he never had any, anyway he was always scouring the papers and news channels for any strange goings on, but nothing materialised, glad to say.'

'And what about the three bodies at the farmhouse?'

'You lot came for them, after all they were your men you sent up.'

'It doesn't mention anything in the file.'

'Didn't think it would, just like I think you are listening to the ramblings of an old man.'

'No, it's not ramblings, we know you are telling the truth.'

Williams looked at them.

'Because we have one.'

'What do you mean, you have one?'

'We captured one, have it in a holding cell.'

Williams didn't respond.

'I have been instructed to ask if you would like to accompany us back.'

'What for?'

'You are the only person that has any knowledge about them, maybe you could help us understand them better.'

'Don't see how.'

'We have had it for two weeks, and it hasn't spoken.'

The tall one retrieved the leather case from the side of the couch and opened it, he passed Williams a photo. Williams looked at it and immediately recognised the picture. The face hadn't grown old like his, she still looked like the person that had saved his life all those decades ago.

'Yes, I will help,' he said.

He wasn't going to help them, but somehow, he knew he needed to do all he could to get her out of that place they had incarcerated her in.

THE END

Printed in Great Britain
by Amazon